W9-ACF-333

INTRUDER IN THE WIND

INTRUDER
IN THE
WIND

by Jess Carr

Commonwealth Press/Virginia

Manufactured in the United States
of America

*For Flossie Mitchell Hart, who bequeathed
to me the stuff of which novelists are made.*

CHAPTER I

The isolated farm was alive with sounds. It was spring, and the air was charged with a perfumed essence; the surrounding forest starting to bud and bloom. Towering hardwood and softwood trees overshadowed clumps of redbud bushes, and at ground level cone-shaped morels, Indian pipe, white trillium, birdfoot violets, bloodroot, and an occasional scarlet lady's slipper completed a colorful and aromatic mosiac. Birds large and small harmonized under a clear blue sky. From a briar thicket a mockingbird flung his chatterings upon the intruder, but the thrushes kept up their carolings. Sparrows chirped here and there, rushing about and casting small shadows against the earth that had long been greening. A sacred robin flew overhead and offered a note passing sweet until the orchestra serenaded fragrant fields and breeze-stirred trees. In a rotting locust tree a large red-headed woodhen, hammering her beak against the bark, played bass and rounded out the ode of joy.

Adam "Spider" Cornett had drunk in this identical sight countless times. Having bought out the shares of his brother and sister, he had finally become sole owner of the family homestead. It wasn't a spread of land that anyone could brag about, for the farm consisted of just 90 acres, and aside from the timber that grew on approximately one half of the acreage, the balance of the land was fit only for grazing sheep. It was doubtful that there was even 10 acres that could be successfully cultivated.

In most any direction the eye wandered, protruding limestone boulders dotted the landscape, and here and there great rock piles attested to the labors and determination of his predecessors to keep the land productive. And even the rock piles were not ordinary rock piles.

Someone had taken the trouble to stack the rocks neatly as though building a sturdy circular stone wall. Within the neat circle, rocks were arched until the pile looked like a haystack. Ever since Spider had heard the country and Western song, *Rocky Top*, he had thought it appropriately descriptive of his land. Even so, he was proud of his modest "estate" and took every opportunity to walk over it and observe the sights and sounds of nature. He earned his living as a miner, and on occasion he would bring friends out to his land for hunting or hiking. He was tall and lanky, and even going up hill his long strides would soon outdistance the best of competitors. Sometimes he could stretch his legs widely enough to step from one limestone outcropping to another, and for a tall man he was surprisingly agile. No doubt it was this observation that had compelled his friends to come up with the nickname, "Spider."

Because of his height, it was well that the era of the pick and shovel miner was gradually disappearing. In no way could he have fit his gangly frame into a narrow mine shaft. But, of course, his father and his grandfather before him had done precisely that, had lain on their sides or crouched on their knees and dug the black rock ton after ton. Now the mines were mechanized, and Spider felt himself fortunate to be a coal cutting machine operator. From Spider's point of view, he doubted that any man or woman—and there were female miners now—ever felt truly comfortable and safe in the dusty tunnels under the earth. Men and women were not moles. They were meant to breathe fresh air and see the sky. Nevertheless, the wages were good, the benefits hard to resist, and the truth was that one quarter of the population of this little town of Corbin, Kentucky, didn't know how to do anything else except dig, shovel, load and haul.

Basking in the knowledge that he could temporarily escape the endless dark tunnels filled with devastating dust and enjoy a walk across his land, Spider struck out for the crest of the hill.

He followed the circling animal trail rather than go straight up, and as he passed between limestone ledges and rotting tree stumps, he glanced backward occasionally at the swaybacked old farm house, now gradually collapsing under its own weight. It was presently, as it had always been, a humble dwelling place. The gray weatherboarding curled ever outwardly toward the sun, as though shedding skin. A hay barn and an outhouse had already collapsed, but the residence was still groaning in its death throes; still home to bats and barn swallows. He had been born in that house 37 years ago, but during the period of prosperity the Korean War era brought on, his father and mother had moved to the town of Corbin, thus allowing their children some of the advantages of life the remoter location would not provide. Here and there in the yard, unkept forsythia and apple japonica bushes bloomed, and beyond the tree line that lay at the structure's west side, dogwood and a few old fruit trees were starting to bloom. He took the sweet aroma of it into his nostrils and continued to look back at the scene with both nostalgia and disappointment. He hadn't wanted his birthplace to decay, but he hadn't the money to support a town house, a wife and two children, and finance a major remodeling job. But someday he would. Someday he would jack up the corners, salvage the skeletal framework, and give the place a whole new interior and exterior. He was ever the dreamer. He had long ago come to terms with that. No place was better for dreaming and fantasizing than the tunnels and pockets and shafts deep under the earth.

At the crown of the hill, Spider looked across a valley, another range of low lying hills, then to the southern outskirts of the town of Corbin. Some would call Corbin a sleepy little place but there had been numerous times across the decades when the town had been anything but that. Corbin's early history was replete with occurrences of feuds, mine wars, union rampages, and the more ordinary drunken brawls on a Saturday night. Outsiders might call the whole county deprived, as indeed they had during the Kennedy years when Appalachia had been rediscovered and labeled a poverty belt from Pennsylvania to Georgia. Most of his friends and neighbors who were old enough to remember those years had expressed a sense of amusement at their "discovery" and wondered why, all of a sudden, they had become the object of national focus. "Politics," most of them were quick to say and, of course, thay had been right. "Deprived" or not, they were all people of common sense and uncanny instincts whether they were well educated or not. After all, their ancestors had come to eastern Kentucky, tamed the wilderness, survived, and sometimes prospered, for 200 years before their Kennedy-era discovery.

Spider stood spellbound with the magnificence of the view. A compelling sense of harmony resonated with the peace in Spider's own soul. The feeling didn't last long, however, because as he allowed his eyes to sweep over the landscape, he saw the distant tipple of Swindoll-Manning Coal Company, his employer. It reminded him that on this day he was starting the three to eleven shift, and it was now almost twelve noon. He drank in the view a bit longer and noticed in the far distance a dirty haze on the horizon. It was unusual that so early in the spring the contaminated air drifted down the Appalachian chain from Pennsylvania. Normally, the stifling overcast did not hit eastern Kentucky at its maximum density until late July and August.

Unexpectedly, an intruding sound broke his reverie. It was the mournful bleating of a lambless ewe. Spider raised sheep on his rocky but rich land, and he had concluded that sheep or goats were about the only thing that could prosper on the steep slopes. He sold lambs and wool and more than offset the upkeep and taxes on the old homestead, and he expected no more than that. But now, perhaps, even that small income was threatened. In the last week, four of his newborn lambs had simply disappeared. In such a remote location, anything could have happened to them. A sheep-killing dog—or a pack of wild dogs—were the most common

4

menace—although on rare occasion local farmers suffered the depredations of a bear. While wolves had plagued the early settlers, they were now a thing of the past.

The lambless ewe kept up her piteous bleating and walked toward him as though to solicit comfort. It was amazing and touching how much the mothers suffered in the loss of their offspring. It would be weeks before the mourning ended. Of course, sometimes when a ewe had twin lambs, he had been successful in getting a lambless ewe to take one of the offspring of another ewe. That little feat was not easy to accomplish because every ewe knew her own lamb by its individual smell. But this year's crop of lambs had produced only four sets of twins. He had bred his ewes late to insure that the lambs would not arrive in the worst part of winter. He could not always get out to the farm during the harsh periods to attend his flock, and thus he had planned his breeding program so that the lambs would arrive in early spring. The mature sheep could withstand any kind of snow and ice that January and February produced. Newborn lambs were another matter: born bloody and wet, the icy winds would freeze them very quickly unless they were inside a barn, and now there was no barn.

Spider knelt and petted all of the sheep that came to him. Most of them had become like pets anyway. The sorrowful voices of the lambless ewes predominated in the flock, but Spider was powerless to assuage their grieving. All the other ewes seemed profoundly content licking their newborns or allowing them to alternately suck and butt their source of milk.

After a few more moments of such communion, Spider stood and headed back. He had brought no feed in his pickup truck, but he did have a block of salt as a peace offering. He marvelled at how much he must look like a shepherd of the ancient lands and times as he walked down the hill, his entire flock following. The newborn lambs were both cute and awkward. They staggered about like a drunk miner on a Saturday night, and their long legs were out of proportion to their small, undeveloped bodies.

He got the block of salt from the pickup and carried it a way up the side of the hill and placed it on a flat rock ledge. The mature sheep took to the offering immediately; the newborn lambs ignorant of the delicacy placed before them. A few of the lambs wandered far afield of their mothers but Spider had no concerns in that regard. A ewe could sort out and find her offspring no matter where or how far she wandered.

Chore done, he headed for the pickup truck, cranked it and started to turn about. His peripheral vision discerned some kind of rapid movement just above the high ground line. He braked to a halt and looked out the side window. In the flash of an instant, a great bird had swooped down, locked its talons in the flesh of an isolated lamb, and lifted the prey into the air. The act of piracy had occurred so quickly that Spider was frozen to the truck seat in disbelief. Quite clearly, the great bird had been a golden eagle. He had seen them before, riding the wind currents up and down the great valleys of eastern Kentucky and Tennessee. He knew also that the theft of baby lambs by eagles was not all that rare in various locations throughout the world. But it was the first time he had observed such a theft.

Unbelievably, no sooner had the thieving eagle flopped across the crest of the hill with its heavy load than he saw a second eagle clear the tree line and start into a dive for a second isolated lamb. Spider knew that it was illegal to shoot the beautiful birds since they were a protected species. Nevertheless, he reached behind him and withdrew his deer rifle from the cab-mounted gun rack and fired a quick shot into the air. The powerful blast echoed from ridge to ridge, and the eagle took off in frantic flight. Spider got off another couple of rounds, this time with the expended bullets coming close enough to the eagle's body that it would feel and hear the hiss of the traveling projectile. Although he couldn't shoot them, maybe they could be scared off permanently.

6

There was a moment of reckoning in his act, however, when Spider realized that rather than solving his problem, he might just be driving the marauders from his own land onto the farm of a neighbor. But at least the mystery had been solved. He now knew where those missing lambs had disappeared to; they had been dropped into the great nests of the eagles on the cliffs and shredded into tender morsels for their young.

CHAPTER II

Joe Fremont watched his wife, Maria, pack his dinner pail and reminded her to put in plenty of dill pickles. He didn't care how crazy it sounded, but the juice of dill pickles was the best of all things to clear coal dust from one's throat. Although he was scheduled to report for the 3 to 11 shift at Swindoll-Manning Coal, he still had a little time to spare, and he drifted from his wife's side to a back bedroom and stood beside his son's bassinet. The truth was, he thought that the state of first-time fatherhood had been invented just for him. He was 26 years old now, a tower of physical strength and unashamedly proud of his muscle hardened body. As he looked down at his sleeping son, Joshua, he was reminded that there had been a time when he doubted the power and virility of the body he had so meticulously cultivated in work and play. For five years after their marriage, Maria had failed to conceive. In those early years, they had missed few nights of lovemaking, and as the months had gone by without a sign of her pregnancy, he had pounded her almost unmercifully in his sense of frustration. He had thought "unmercifully" but Maria was as receptive to his superhuman efforts as he was to expend them.

When they both had realized their efforts were futile and agreed to seek medical help, for a time he had gone into the deepest depression of his life. The mere thought that their childlessness could be laid at his door was more than he could bear. If it was his fault, he had visions of the word getting out, and his having to walk a gauntlet down the main shaft of the mine. And, of course, every fellow miner and mechanic would be lined up on each side jeering at him as he fled them in shame and humiliation. But he had escaped that imagined torment, for after the series of medical tests and examinations he and his wife had endured, it was determined that Maria was the barren one, having been deprived of motherhood because of blocked tubes. It was Maria who had suffered, then. Her lithe body had shook uncontrollably in his arms when she had received the news. Once he'd seen her in the distance pounding her chest with her fists as though to punish her full breasts for being milkless.

But all that was old history. Now, sleeping peacefully in the bassinet before his eyes was their miracle baby. And Maria was more beautiful than she had ever been. He wondered how that was possible, and yet it was. Since that first day he had met her—just a year out of high school—he had thought her the most beautiful girl on the face of the earth. And she hadn't been what the boys at the mine called a "coal field queen." The coal field queens had a way of reminding you at every corner and turn that they were "it on a stick." They all seemed to know the same regulation jiggle and exciting ripple of body language, and a particular glint in the eyes that seemed to say, "How can you possibly resist wanting some?"

No, Maria hadn't been like that, not that he was immune to the tantalizing charms of coal field queens. He'd had his share, and he'd also had his share of hero worship in his own right. He'd been the star fullback on the Corbin County High School football team, and he'd come within a gnat's eyebrow of getting a college scholarship for his athletic prowess. But in the end, it hadn't worked out and he bummed around for a year before capitulating like most everyone else he knew to life in the mines. At first, he had hated his job and showed his rebellion over loss of the scholarship by spending his off hours in brawls and drunken parties. In those days, he had loved a good fight. He didn't mind, even, feeling a fist slam into his own jaw and tasting his own salty blood in his mouth, for it was always an invitation to respond in like manner.

9

There was something in his psyche that revelled in violence. At athletic events—both when he played and now as an observer—the excitement was greatest when the contest was most brutal; even when people were injured and blood flowed. Fist fights had occurred more than once during and after Corbin games. There were times that he questioned this aspect of himself and those same traits in his friends and neighbors. What was in him—them—that demanded eruption on occasion? Did they all have some historic carryover from their ax and rifle-wielding predecessors who had cut their way through Cumberland Gap, opened up the great wilderness road, and overcome the bears, wolves, dense forest, and hostile Indians of eastern Kentucky and Tennessee? Maybe it wasn't that at all. Maybe it was that his forebears had been so poor, isolated, and unschooled that they had invented their own mores and formulated their own culture. Heaven knew the area was historically replete with Hatfield-McCoy type feuds, company versus union wars, murders on a whim or for the sheer hell of it. Even the mines were vast dark wombs where men seemed to be conceived and expurgated every day; not a new birth exactly, but one in which the offspring were daily a little sicker, a little angrier, and a little nearer death from dust or gas or the cold sweats of fear.

But on a personal level things were different now. Even before their marriage, Maria, with angelic patience and love, had endured his periods of depression, violence, and excessive drinking. Once, he had nearly lost her when on a boozing binge with some buddies he had taken up with one of the coal field queens for a couple of weekends. He had learned the hard way that she was no coal town Pollyanna. But such defensive outbursts from her were rare. She had changed him by her very character, and she had done it so skillfully that to this day he couldn't figure out the exact methods of her reformation of him. There was a sweetness in her that was as natural as her beauty. She was tall, and blessed with the most luxurious head of ash blood hair he had ever seen. She possessed that most delightful of physical combinations; a lithe body perfectly proportioned, with full breasts and a swan-like neck that he loved to hold in both of his large hands as he kissed her.

Having her—loving her—had changed his entire outlook on life; had changed his own personality and given him greater self confidence, greater peace of mind, and an overall feeling of optimism. He had been promoted to chief maintenance electrician in the mines as a result, and as demanding and dangerous as his job sometimes was, there were times that he had moments of total distraction just thinking about her and wished to throw down his tools and run home to make wild passionate love even if it was the middle of the afternoon. He knew that he couldn't express it in any really poetic way, but making love to Maria was akin to that first time he'd drunk a full glass of moonshine. He'd been only 14 then, but he remembered it well. First there was the anticipation. Then, he had sipped on the fiery liquid and felt his flesh grow gradually warm. As though his blood was overheating too fast, his vision had blurred a little bit, and he had the sensation that his eyes were crossing. Not long thereafter, he had the most infinite sense of peace, and it was as though his mind was floating free of his body. He had sworn that he could hear birds singing and the buzz of bees about his ears, but maybe he'd been brainwashed. The makers of the powerful brew had assured him that the sunshine itself and the perfume of mountain honeysuckle were in the jar. Even in retrospect, he didn't like to remember what the night and the next day were like. There had been the devil to pay when his head had felt as though someone had sunk a woodsman's ax into his skull, and his belly had become a great volcano, purging itself of boulders and molten lava. But, yes, up to the point when bad things started to happen, making love to Maria was just like that.

Having finished packing his pail, Maria came and stood at his side. As they always did while viewing their child together, their arms lapped around each other.

"He's sleeping so peacefully," Maria said.

"Yeah. I'd like to be sacked out like that myself. Ought to get the little freeloader a pick and shovel and put him to work."

His jest brought Maria's hand up from his waist, and she pounded him on the shoulder with a balled-up fist.

"You wouldn't dare even if he were 16 years old. Besides, Joshua is going to be a bank president some day—not a coal miner."

With his index finger, Joe touched his son lightly and traced a line down across the infant's cheek. Three weeks previously, this child had been born small and a little frail, but now Joshua had started to fill out. Prior to fatherhood, Joe had not known that a washed clean infant emitted a pleasing aroma. He bent down further and took a deeper whiff.

"He can't need changing again," Maria said.

"Not that. I just like to smell him when he's pink and clean. I wish you'd wake him and nurse him before I leave," Joe said but avoided his wife's eyes.

Finally, he did turn and look her way, and there was a look of mysterious mirth in Maria's great brown eyes. He'd always thought that her eyes looked like those of a doe—intelligent and soft. Never in her life would he tell her this, but once during hunting season, he had raised his sights to fell a fat doe, but while looking into the animal's eyes, he had faltered and lowered his rifle. The animal's eyes were too much like those of his wife.

Maria turned and kissed her husband quickly.

"What if it gets you all excited and then you have to rush off to work?" she asked with the same intensified gleam in her eyes.

"Well, this time it'll have to wait."

She lifted the baby from his bassinet, sat in the bedroom rocker, and started to arouse him slowly. Joshua's little pink lips started in half conscious motion, then he turned his face and began to nuzzle. Maria unbuttoned her blouse and loosened the flaps of her nursing bra. Something about that approach this time was unsatisfactory to Joe, and he reached behind her and unsnapped her bra. She got the message and finished the rest of the maneuver herself while balancing the baby in first one arm, then the other.

Her full breasts, swollen even larger now with milk, excited him to a degree that he could never explain in volumes of words. But it was more than sexual excitement. Seeing his child "eat" was a picture rare and beautiful. He wondered whether or not the sense of joy and well being that his wife obviously felt while nursing their son could possibly be any greater than his own. There was magic in it.

Joshua sucked hungrily, and Maria set her rocking chair in motion. Maria's free breast began to dribble milk, and Joe reached to chair side, retrieved a tissue, and dabbled at the moisture. The previous night in his hunger to make love to her—yet knowing that such was not permissible yet—his lips had tunneled their way to one of her nipples. He had thus tasted the sweet nectar of her breast, and the spontaneous act had been both a strange and exciting experience. But Maria had withdrawn from him quickly as though he intruded on forbidden ground. Even so, the moment had given him something special and memorable. And if it was possible, he had reached a new plateau of love for his wife.

Maria switched the infant to her other breast. It wasn't long, however, until his little belly was full and content. With the nipple still in his mouth, he was fast asleep with surplus milk oozing down the side of his chin. Maria put the child back in his bassinet, covered him with a blanket, and started to get her own clothing back in order. For a moment, Joe restrained her.

"I like goin' to work with this kind of an inspiration," he said with a sheepish grin.

"I have a feeling that if the doctor had given us the go-ahead, you might just be late for work today."

"Not much doubt about that. I'd better hit the road now," he said with a sigh and gave her a peck on the cheek.

13

She didn't let him get away with such a listless farewell, and she locked her arms around his waist. She loved the feeling of wrapping her arms round his big body and feeling the ripple of muscle against her forearms. There was power in him and power in reserve. He wasn't an educated man, and yet he was wise with a sensitivity toward her and her son that he would be ashamed of showing to anyone else. As they stood, she let her lips graze the hollow of his neck, but his day-old beard felt like splinters against her tongue. She backed away, ran her fingers through his wiry red hair, and looked into intense eyes that were as gray as the slate that overhung the mine shafts. "You and I? We've got something special. I wouldn't ever want to lose that," she said.

"Yeah. We got something special."

She kissed her husband hard, handed him his pail, and saw him through the kitchen door. She had to grin. He walked as though he still wore his football uniform. He weighed 216 lbs. now, just a bit over the trim 194 lbs. he had weighed as a fullback. Of course, she knew that the after-work beers had done that for him. Even so, he was still firm all over, not suffering from the "dunlap's disease" (done lapped over his belt).

She lingered at the doorway until his truck had cleared the long driveway of their two acres of ground, and when he looked back to wave, she waved in return, smiling.

Joe Fremont was an enigma if there ever was one. He was every inch the mountain man, full of prejudices, hatreds, and with a potential for violent response. But there was a gentleness in him too; a love for nature, a fierce sense of independence, and a basic belief in the Creator. She knew that she had been successful in helping him to build upon his assets and to curb his liabilities. Even so, there were some things about him that still annoyed her. In private, no man could be more loving and sensitive to her needs. In public, however, he was careful to guard his affection. Even around his own family or hers, he displayed this same guardedness. What

14

was it about mountain men—or men with a mountain heritage—which never allowed them to show to the world that they loved their women? Was it, in their eyes at least, supposed to be a sign of weakness? If so, how did it diminish a man if the world knew he adored his wife?

Her family had not been natives of Eastern Kentucky. Her father, a sales representative for a mining machinery manufacturer, had been transferred to the state during her latter two years of high school. The truth was, her parents felt that she married "down," and that she should have disdained marriage to a common coal miner and gone on to a four year college. Her father had now been transferred to Pennsylvania, so it had been a while since she'd heard that replay of a broken record. But since the day she'd met him, she had never wanted anything so much as she'd wanted Joe Fremont. Even so, she had been level-headed enough to know that it was wise to learn a profession of some sort. Women needed to be able to support themselves and to have a professional interest of their own. Besides, in Corbin, and mining towns elsewhere, there was a more practical reason: collapsing mines and death by flooding and poison gas created a frightening mortality rate among the male population. She could hardly bring herself to think about such things, but it was possible the day might come when she'd have to be self sustaining. She had thus gone off to beautician's school and had returned to Corbin to become an employee of May's Beauty Salon. Two months after her and Joe's wedding, she had been made assistant manager at the salon.

She well knew the stereotype of the average beautician. Such a person—according to the stereotype—was supposed to be a gossipy, gum chewing chatterbox with her nose always into other people's business. Maria could hardly deny that such gathering places didn't invite gossip as well as more serious topics, but just as often she had heard matters of national defense, the peace movement, and national and local politics discussed with insight and intelligence. Somehow, however, juicy tidbits

15

from this or that patron did manage to take precedence. But Maria prided herself in the fact that most times she could simply listen and in good grace remain neutral. It was impossible not to hear—or hear of—all the local gossip, but basking in the exotic and intriguing nature of it was something she had tried hard to avoid. She was top flight in her profession, and a part of her self-discipline was trying daily to improve upon her performance. She couldn't remember the days when beehive hairdos were the rage, and when teasing was an art unto itself. The greatest joy of all was in seeing a woman get up from her chair fully confident that Maria had somehow worked a miracle.

There came a day, however, when Maria had suffered in the company of some of her patrons. Her disquiet had come with the presence of those customers who were in advanced pregnancy. Allowing themselves just a decent time interval so that the fingers of gossip could not be pointed at Joe and herself, Maria had tried to become pregnant quickly. Month after month it hadn't worked and the sight of a pregnant woman in Maria's chair, or even on the street, drove Maria to fits of depression. She had always loved children. Even while in elementary school, the opportunity to hold a squirming infant sent shivers of joy through her young body. Back then, she had watched older women nurse and longed for the time she could hold her own child at her breast and in her arms.

But that building resentment she had for the lucky women whose bellies and breasts were swollen in anticipation of motherhood had turned out in a way not anticipated. In her darkest moments Maria could have imagined them sneering at her barrenness while they gloried in their fertility. But the paradox of the people of Corbin was that while they had the capacity for feuding, pettiness, biases and prejudices, they ultimately revealed a big and loving heart as well. When finally she and Joe had both undergone extensive physical checkups and determined the source of their childlessness, Maria had found the courage to share with her coworkers and a few patrons her problem and great disappointment. Not until still later had she shared with this same group that she might become pregnant by in vitro fertilization. But that process was out of the question. Their doctor had been candid enough to tell them that such a route was not the way poor people could easily go. The cost, he'd said, was $5,000 for each attempted in vitro fertilization, and that many women who'd ultimately been successful in becoming pregnant that way had required two, three, or four fertilization procedures. Joe had checked with his personnel office at the mines to determine whether or not his insurance policy would cover such a procedure, and, of course, it would not. Nevertheless, Maria could not let the dream die. Each time a pregnant woman came into the beauty shop, Maria somehow felt diminished and sad.

Someone in town—or at her place of employment—and to this day she did not know who, had seen her agony and had done something about it. Quite out of the blue, a fund had been started and it was well under way before Maria or Joe was even aware of it. Nevertheless, within a sixty day period, Maria was presented by two of her coworkers with the first proceeds of the fund which totalled $3,627.17. With the delivery of the money into her own hands, uncharacteristically, Maria had wept with such emotion that she had spilled the entire bankroll onto the floor of the beauty shop.

By the time her physician had set up the appointment, and she and Joe had prepared themselves to journey to Norfolk, Virginia, where the in vitro fertilization procedure would take place, the fund had grown to over $5,200. It was enough money for the first fertilization attempt plus help with traveling expenses there and back. She remembered that day when they had driven out of Corbin, and she had wanted to double back and wrap her arms around the whole town and the people who lived there, and to tell them how much she loved them.

In retrospect, she had envisioned herself and Joe returning triumphant to Corbin some weeks later, announcing that she was pregnant at last. It hadn't been that simple. The in vitro fertilization had failed. Yet nobody had given her time to be depressed and without hope. The fund raising had started all over again. Donations came in in pennies, dollars, $10 and $20 dollar bills, and checks. An anonymous donation of $500 was the icing on the cake that had again brought the total fund to just over the $5,000 mark.

This time she had come back to Corbin triumphant. The second attempt had been successful and she enjoyed a glorious pregnancy free of serious illness or complications. She had insisted upon a natural birth, and when she had squeezed her baby from her womb and it had been held by its heels for her viewing, again she had wept for joy. Thus had the miracle baby come into the world.

Seemingly, half of the population of Corbin had claimed partial parentage. It was funny but when friends or strangers approached her on the street to inquire of little Joshua, she wondered whether they owned $2 or $20 dollars' worth of him. On the street or in the stores, children, too, approached her, especially if Joshua was with her. No doubt, they had heard the story of the miracle baby from their parents, and perhaps they, too, had dipped into their piggy bank and donated their pennies, nickels, and dimes.

CHAPTER III

Joshua awoke shortly after four, and Maria could tell from his protests that he needed changing. Was it her imagination, or, already, could she discern his needs by the modulation and timbre of his cries? After she had pinned on fresh diapers, she went through her little ritual of tickling his tummy and lowering her head so that her ash blonde locks could fall in his face, thus initiating a quick churning of his stubby arms and legs. She could swear that she had evoked first a grin and then an attempted cry of delight from him. She picked him up and walked back to the kitchen. The window over her kitchen sink faced the west, and the westernly-leaning sun was framed in the opening. She remembered how delightfully sunny it was when she'd seen Joe out to his truck. As a matter of fact, the entire week had been exceptionally warm for early spring.

On an impulse, she took her child back into his room, put a warm shirt on him, and wrapped him in a blanket.

"How about a bit of sunshine today, my little man?" she cooed. "And some fresh air won't hurt you either."

Bundle in arms, Maria exited the house and stepped into the bright out-of-doors. The sunrays felt good on her bare arms, and she peeled Joshua's blanket back so that his body, too, might feel the toasty warmth. The glare played havoc with Joshua's tiny brownish eyes—her eyes, everyone said—and Maria shielded his face with her hand for a moment of adjustment.

Holding the child tightly, Maria pirouetted for a distance across the lush green grass. She noted that it would soon need cutting. It was just one more proof that summer was on the way. Her flower borders had already come alive with blooming jonquils, crocus, and other early flowers. Here and there within the spacious lawn, the bright yellow of forsythia bushes contrasted nicely against the green grass, and the pinkish-red of apple japonica bushes complemented the gray bark of shade trees.

Along the west property line of their small two acre plot, Joe had established a garden. Maria walked in that direction, noting as she approached the site how dead vines and plants from the previous growing season looked stark against the uneven soil. Soon, however, their next door neighbor, Dowless Anthony, would come and plow, and the aroma of freshly turned earth would be another ritual of spring. Dowless never rested, and it seemed that he was into everything. Aside from his job at the mines and his supervision of the Swindoll-Manning Coal Company Mine Safety and Rescue Service, he plowed gardens for a fee in the spring, baled hay in the summer, and cut firewood for sale in the fall and winter.

Maria was proud of her modest home and grounds. To be sure, it was no showplace, but it was clean and neat inside and out, and with its white clapboard construction, painted green roof, with green shutters to match, it was compatible with the landscape. The one-story structure boasted five spacious rooms and a full basement, and already Joe had talked about sectioning off a portion of the basement as a playroom for Joshua. What her home lacked in finery was more than made up for in the exquisiteness of the view. Their two acres crowned the highest hill on the south side of town. On a clear day, like today, she could see all the way into the adjoining county of Whitley where the King's Rest Mountains formed the backdrop. Those craggy pedestals of limestone looked little more than sand castles from Maria's vantage point, but viewed closer up along Interstate 75 they were formidable columns of boulders stacked upon boulders until they towered literally into the heavens.

Drinking it all in, she turned her eyes skyward and tilted Joshua's wobbly head upward as though he could really be her viewing companion. The sky looked more robin-egg blue than cyan, and to the north and east, small irregularly shaped clouds seemed to float like sail boats across a calm sea. She turned her vision southward again where the view was most limitless. Crows and hawks and smaller birds flew effortlessly from ridge to ridge, and at various places on the mountains, she could make out specks of white and magenta. The white would be the blooms of wild dogwood, of course, and the brighter shades would be redbud or what the natives called "Judas trees." With her head still held high, she took in a deep breath of the pure air and said a prayer. How could anyone be more blessed than she? Her sense of gratitude actually sent little tremors through her body, and again she pirouetted with her child held tightly in her arms. Everything seemed so perfectly harmonious, but no sooner had she thought that than little changes began to take place. A puff of warm wind rattled the leafless limbs of trees and a broken branch fell to the ground. In the sky, the birds and crows and hawks she had observed earlier had suddenly taken rapid flight as though to seek sanctuary.

The warm breeze stilled, and the sun felt hotter than ever. Perhaps it was only because the winter had been so long and so cold, but never had the soothing sunrays felt so welcome. Maria pirouetted again with her child to the barest, sunniest section of the lawn and sat down in the grass. She spread out Joshua's blanket beside her and laid him on his back. The glare of the sun was soon offensive to the child, and she turned him over on his stomach. She could see him straining to raise his little head, and she marvelled at his determination.

"Not for a while yet, sweetheart," she cooed.

He didn't give up easily, and she thought the exercise would be good for him. With the flat of her hand under his belly, she assisted him until it looked as though he was actually doing push-ups. Although he now weighed over eight pounds, he still felt light in her palm. The sun gave a bright sheen to the child's silky, strawberry blonde hair, and a healthy pink glow to his soft flesh. She could only stare and marvel at this most miraculous of miracles. Every inch of her son seemed to be alive with activity and muscle flexing. He was clearly enjoying the outing as much as she did.

A faint ringing noise in the distance interrupted the special moment. She listened intently and discerned that the sound was coming through the opened door into her kitchen. She decided just to let it ring. It had seemed that every day friends and strangers alike had phoned for a progress report on her child. She couldn't be angry. After all, in a way most unique, many had a hand in making Joshua's birth a reality. The phone continued to ring. The longer she ignored it, the more uncomfortable she felt. It was the miner's wife syndrome again. Every miner's wife had to live with the fact that one day she might receive a phone call reporting a blow-up or a cave-in or some other catastrophe at the mine.

She hopped up quickly, took a few steps, and looked back at her child. He was truly enjoying himself and she let him lie. She ran for the kitchen door and lunged for the phone. The voice was that of her mother-in-law, and for a moment Maria was annoyed.

Maggie Fremont was not the easiest of women to get on with, but Maria had long ago figured out that her mother-in-law's wide mood swings and erratic temperament were not without reason. The woman had lost both her eldest son and her husband to the ravenous belly of separate mines. Maggie just wanted to talk, and Maria listened. As everybody did, she wanted a progress report on her newest grandchild, and while watching Joshua through the kitchen window, Maria provided a cheerful update. That update was all Maria was able to utter; the older woman was soon off in another conversational direction. While Maggie Fremont chatted on, Maria unraveled the long extension cord and made her way to the refrigerator. She poured herself a glass of orange juice and repositioned herself before the kitchen window. She started to raise the glass to her lips.

Glass crashing into the sink and her own screech were simultaneous. Maggie Fremont was soon screaming into the phone, "What is it, what is it?"

Maria's breath deserted her, and her heart seemed to stop. She flung the receiver into the sink and ran for the door. Had her senses deserted her or had she really seen a monstrous bird make an exploratory pass at her child lying helplessly upon his blanket?

No sooner had her racing feet cleared the threshold than she knew she wasn't having a nightmare. Like a dive bomber the great bird was in such a powerful downward plunge that she could hear the hiss of the wind slide past its body. For a brief second, she had halted, mesmerized, but she was quickly running and screaming in the direction of her child.

"Get away! Get away!" she shrieked louder as she ran, but the big bird's concentration on his evil mission seemed unbreakable.

Long before she could close the remaining distance between her child and herself, the bird had outstretched its legs like the landing gear of an aircraft, locked its talons into the flesh of the child, and lifted it into the air so effortlessly that it defied her belief. For a split second, she could not even yell again. What she had just witnessed was so unreal that she questioned her sanity. Then, mournful cries were coming staccato from her throat.

Dowless Anthony, their next door neighbor, literally jumped the fence between their two properties and was quickly at her side. Even after he had taken her shoulders in his strong hands and shaken her, she still could not find voice to tell him what had happened. Her terror-filled, flooding eyes could only stare into the sky. Finally, she pointed. The bird was circling with its heavy load as though it had taken off into the wind, gained a little altitude, and now began a heading for home.

Dowless could now see the problem for himself, but what he saw was unbelievable. The feathered marauder was clearly a golden eagle. No other bird traversing the mountains of Kentucky could match that size and power.

The circling eagle was now on a straight path, and as it passed overhead, Dowless could see the wailing infant being lifted higher and higher. The baby was being carried perpendicular to the eagle's head and thus the talons appeared to be sunk into the buttocks and upper shoulder of the infant's body. Dowless breathed a sigh of relief for that blessing. Had the talons been sunk into the small—or upper—back and into the neck where the spinal cord most likely would have been punctured, the child would already be dying.

Maria's agony was now a combination of shrieks, wails, and sporadic weeping, and she tried to cling to him. He pushed her away and hopped back over the fence. His side vision caught her falling onto the grass and groveling like a wounded animal.

Dowless ran for his company truck. As soon as his radio came alive and he had contacted the Mine Safety and Rescue Service dispatcher, Dowless practically screamed into the mike.

"Who's on duty? Who's on duty?"

"It's me—Danny, Dowless. You mean to tell me all the elbow bendin' me and you have done together, you don't recognize my voice—"

"Cut the crap, Danny. We've got an emergency on our hands. Which of our copters is on the ground?"

"Only the Hughes. We sent the Jet Ranger up to Louisville this morning for some engine repair. What's the problem?"

"No time to explain. Get that Hughes in the air immediately and don't waste a second. I'll instruct the pilot the minute he's airborne. I'll be standin' by."

"Yes, sir. On the double!"

Dowless looked southward. The eagle and its prey were now getting smaller and smaller, but he could still see them clearly. The eagle's great wings were laboring with the drag of its burden. A terrible thought occurred to him. What if the eagle tired of the weight locked in its talons and simply decided to drop the infant? Undoubtedly, the eagle was headed for the King's Rest mountain range, the highest point in the area. It would be a natural point of hiding for the eagle and any brothers and sisters the magnificent bird might have. But if he had guessed correctly, that eagle had a long way to fly. One thing was certain: He didn't have to second guess what that eagle wanted with a tender infant. The chances were good there were half a dozen eagles' nests lodged at the crown of King's Mountain. Joshua Fremont would soon be nothing more than shredded meat for a nest full of baby eagles.

Dowless saw the Company chopper rise above the tree line, and he rushed back to his radio. When he was bridged into the cockpit of the Hughes, he didn't give the pilot, Loopy Elmore, time to ask any questions.

"Loopy, can you see a big bird—an eagle—floppin' through the air? He's flyin' slow. The load he's carryin' is Maria and Joe Fremont's baby. . ."

". . .Saint Gawd!"

"I'll explain what happened later, but right now we've got to move fast. I want you to follow that eagle at a safe distance. Don't you get too close, now, or you'll scare him into droppin' his load. The minute that eagle gets to his nest and releases the child, I want you to hover down close. As soon as we know the baby is restin' safely in the nest, I want you to hover and scare that eagle away. The downwash of air from your rotor should keep the mature eagles away from the area."

"Roger," Loopy confirmed. "But you haven't thought of something; if that baby rolls over on its back—or even if it's on its stomach and its face is pointed in the direction of them baby eagles, those birds will peck its eyes out. Maybe even peck holes in its skin and it'll bleed to death."

Yes, Dowless had thought of those possibilities, but they were too horrible to dwell upon. There was no doubt in his mind whatsoever that the eagle had carried the child face down. The infant would thus be lowered into the eagle's nest face down, and the only luck that he asked for—prayed for—was that the baby eagles would be to one side of the nest with the infant occupying the other side, and his face turned to the rim of the nest itself. Hopefully, the baby eagles would not yet be mature enough that their beaks could really puncture the infant's flesh. If rescue of the child was possible at all, which Dowless seriously doubted, no doubt Joshua's tender flesh would look as though it had been pelted with bird shot. Even if the baby eagles couldn't penetrate the flesh, most certainly they would peck away in the attempt.

There were a few seconds more of silence, and then Dowless barked into the mike, "Got him in your sights, Loopy?"

"Yeah. He's one hell of a specimen. Beautiful. Looks like he's got an eight foot wingspan. He looks and flies like he's king of the mountain or somethin'."

"Maybe the downwash from your rotor will keep even the baby eagles from tryin' any funny business," Dowless said more hopefully than realistically.

"Maybe, but I can't hover this thing forever. There're no gas stations up here, and I don't have more than two or three hours worth of fuel. What's your backup plan?"

"My plan is to get another chopper on the scene. If I can get one with a rescue hoist, maybe we can save that baby's life by lowerin' a man to the nest, restealin' the child, and take him back to his mother. I got my doubts that we'll be takin' her back a live child, but I hope to God we can. You hang in there now. I'm goin' to get on the phone and see how quickly I can get you relieved. It's all in your hands for awhile."

"I hear you."

"I just thought of one more thing," Dowless said. "You got to be mighty careful not to throw too much downwash against that nest. You get too much of a draft hittin' it, and you might dislodge it."

"Got ya."

"Just as a backup measure, I'm goin' to call the state police, the sheriff's department, and the county rescue squad. There's a chance I can get a state police chopper on the scene, but if it's tied up and I have trouble gettin' one from another source, we can get a small army into the mountains and maybe climb up to that nest and do the rescue work ourselves."

"From the looks of things up here," Loopy said, "there's no access roads into the area any closer than ten to fifteen miles. That's a lot of ground to cover on foot."

Dowless wasn't hearing anything he didn't know already. He knew this entire section of Kentucky very well. Those craggy, forbidding mountains were like a kingdom unto itself. Interstate 75 paralleled the range, but the nearly vertical ascent of rock face would defy ordinary men and maybe, even, not a few mountain climbers.

"You're probably right," Dowless agreed after a few moments of thought. "There's no way rescue teams can get up there til long after dark. I'm not sure I can lead a team in there myself at night."

"Then you better hope you can get that big chopper. But you better get it in a hurry. It's not goin' to be any easy thing lowerin' a man in a basket to pick up that kid in daylight much less nighttime. I can tell you somethin' right now; the wind is going' to be fierce up on top of that mountain peak, and a rescue cable and a basket with a man in it is goin' to bobble around like a gas-filled balloon."

Dowless removed his baseball cap and scratched his balding head. "You're not tellin' me anythin' I don't know," he growled. "Maybe we can get a state police chopper or one from somewhere else in a hurry. Hell of a time to have our own Jet Ranger in for an engine overhaul."

"Maybe they haven't started on it yet. Maybe we could get it back down from Louisville."

"Good thinkin'," Dowless said. "It's worth a try. I'm goin' to sign off now. Got things to do. I'll keep you advised. Hang in there."

Dowless used his truck radio to contact the sheriff's department and the county rescue squad. He knew that he could count on a portion of the mine safety and rescue service as well, but a number of the members would have to be kept in reserve against the chance of a mine emergency. He called his dispatcher back and laid out the plan. Every volunteer available would rendezvous at the intersection of 25E and 459 where they would then proceed through Bryant Store and Gausdale, and on by foot to the final destination. The one-half-hour ready time was not much notice, but if he could get a dozen men on the scene early, it might be better than 200 later.

He couldn't reach the state police headquarters by his radio, and he cradled the mike. He'd have to go back, check on Maria, and use her telephone.

When he returned to the Fremont's house, a surprising number of people had already gathered on the lawn. No doubt Maria's screams and shrieks had brought nearby neighbors on the run. The grapevine and telephone lines had obviously allowed the news to spread quickly.

Maria was standing under her own power, but occasionally this person or that would go to her side, plant a kiss upon her cheek, and embrace her. Clearly she fought hard for self control, but even so, uncontrollable sobs would rack her body and cause her eyes to flood again. Dowless walked right into the midst of comforters and told Maria what had already been done. Much to his relief, her face brightened with his assurances that everything was being done that could be done, and that the chances were at least even that they could get her baby back again and quite possibly, alive.

"But why my baby?" Maria wailed. "Why little Joshua?"

"Nearly every year eagles steal newborn lambs somewhere around the area," an elderly man offered. "I've heard about it, and it was in the papers a few days ago."

"But Joshua is so helpless—so innocent," Maria rejected the information.

"But an eagle ain't particular," the old man insisted, "or maybe he don't know the difference. Warm red meat is warm red meat."

For a certainty, the old man didn't mean to be cruel, but the validity of his assertion only made Maria weep all the more.

Dowless had his own theories, but he didn't voice them. He would guess that an eagle selected prey either by visible movement, body radiation of heat, or by smell. Eagles were known to capture just about anything that was warm and that moved. Joshua's blanket still lay in the grass where the baby had lain upon it. He could easily envision the child flexing its arms or legs or turning its head, and how open to the bright sun it had been. Even so, he would have guessed that the odor of a human might be offensive to an eagle, or at least incompatible with its taste buds. A startling thought registered. Was it possible that Maria had oiled down Joshua with lanolin-based lotion: Lanolin being fat extracted from sheep's wool? He had never heard of the capture of an infant by an eagle. That was not to say that it hadn't happened many times. These facts set his mind to thinking again. In reality, he knew little about eagles and their habits and general nature. Perhaps he should call an ornithologist at some nearby university to find out a few things.

When Maria seemed to be calming again, Dowless gave her the additional good news that at this very moment, an advance rescue team was being assembled, and in less than an hour would be on their way to the King's Rest Mountain Range.

"I want Joe," Maria sobbed, but she was under better control now.

"We've already sent into the mine for him," Dowless assured her. "It'll take a while to find him and get him out, but you just hang on."

Dowless turned on his heel and headed for the kitchen. Maria was practically smothered in the sympathy and concern of neighbors, and he could do nothing more for her.

The receiver of the phone still lay in the kitchen sink amid broken glass and the sticky residue of orange juice. No doubt she had flung it there upon seeing the quick descent of the eagle. From the window, the child's blanket looked like a miniature floating pool of aqua against the dark green of the grass.

Dowless reached for the dishcloth and wiped the receiver clean. He looked up the number and dialed the Kentucky State Police headquarters, and to his utter amazement, they had no helicopter of any size or type to offer. But the officer with whom Dowless spoke had one very helpful suggestion: on many occasions the Kentucky State Police had called on the Air National Guard for assistance. The National Guard did have rescue type helicopters. Dowless asked the officer the proper person to call and also that the state police back up his call with an appeal of their own.

"How do I know you're not some kind of a nut?" the officer asked candidly. "The theft of a baby by an eagle sounds pretty wild."

Dowless gave a quick resume of his mine rescue service work and suggested that state police headquarters confirm it, and also that they confirm it with the Corbin Sheriff's Office. Perhaps by the sense of emergency that Dowless was able to convey, the officer either believed him or was at least willing to go along pending his own confirmation of the situation.

Dowless dialed the phone number the state police had given him—a Lexington, Kentucky, area code—and managed by a few choice curse words and a convincing portrayal of what had happened in Corbin, to get through a minor bureaucracy to the officer of the day. The state police were sympathetic compared to the cock and bull he started to receive from the Air National Guard officer.

"I know you don't send choppers out to chase birds," Dowless was almost screaming into the phone, "but an eagle stealin' a child is hardly an everyday incident!"

As though the officer had not fully understood the first time, he became a bit more sympathetic but still noncommittal. Dowless told the officer that the NG would be getting a call from the Kentucky State Police supporting his request.

Dowless hung up and looked at his watch. It was now ten after five. They had little more than three hours of daylight left, and rendezvous time with the search forces was only fifteen minutes away. One thing still remained, and Dowless thought it might be important. He picked up the telephone receiver again and asked the operator for emergency assistance. He told her what he needed, and she suggested the University of Kentucky at Lexington and put him through.

They could not reach the head of the department of ornithology, but a certain Dr. Basil Lawrence was soon on the line. When Dowless related the problem as quickly and concisely as he could, the professor was at first unbelieving.

"I've never heard of such a thing," Lawrence steadfastly maintained. "Rabbits, chickens, even lambs and other small animals sometimes, but infants. . ."

". . .damn it, I'm tellin' you what did happen," Dowless insisted. "Now is there anything you can tell us that we should know about the behavior of these big birds? If worse comes to worse, is there any kind of powder or chemical we could drop from a helicopter on the nests to keep the mature eagles from coming back? Of course, it would have to be some kind of dust that would not injure the child but be offensive to the birds. Can you help us with any information?"

The professor seemed to stammer for a full ten seconds.

"What you call the golden eagle is really the E. chrysaatos," the professor began. "Its nest will be a collection of sticks and grasses usually found on the very pinnacle of cliffs or in the branches of tall trees. They return to the same place year after year and lay from one to four eggs."

"I don't want to enroll in your class, Dr. Lawrence. I guess at this point all I want to know is whether or not that eagle will tear and eat human flesh? I'd like to know, too, why that eagle got so brave and decided to dive into a thickly inhabited area? I know that when wild animals get rabies, they become very brave and seem not to be fearful of the human presence. Are such diseases common to eagles?"

31

Again, there was a moment of indecisive muttering.

"Birds are subject to many diseases, just as all wildlife," Dr. Lawrence finally said. "I guess I will need to do a little research before I can answer most of your questions."

"There isn't time for that. We've got a search team headed for the mountains in the next ten minutes. This is a life and death matter. Can you at least tell me this: do the baby eagles most likely in the nest with the child have sufficient strength to peck the infant to death or to wound him mortally?"

He could hear the professor gulp. "Yes," Dr. Lawrence said firmly, "if they've reached a certain level of maturity. But if luck is with you, there may be only one eaglet in the nest. If the infant's face is turned away from the immature bird, he can survive the minor injuries inflicted."

"But what about dust or spray?" Dowless reiterated.

"Absolutely nothing that I can think of that would not injure the child. I wish that I could do more to help," Dr. Lawrence's voice had a hollow ring.

"Thanks, but I guess it's all our ball of wax now," Dowless signed off and had a feeling that his voice sounded even more hollow.

When Dowless went back out into the yard, the crowd had grown even larger. There was a confusing aura of sympathy, anger, and fear in the mixture of expressions and excited voices. Maria had grown less weepy, but her eyes had the dull look of escalating shock in them. He wondered if she should not be taken to a doctor and he suggested it before departing for the rendezvous. Maria herself shook off the suggestion.

"I'm not moving from this spot until Joe gets here," she said.

Dowless took a friend aside and asked her to call the family physician and have him come to the house.

As Dowless raced again for his truck, new arrivals screeched to a halt in front of the house. The press had arrived, and so had a T.V. mobile camera crew. He

32

climbed into his truck and burned rubber. A glance at his watch told him that he was going to be five minutes late for the rendezvous. They'd wait for him, and maybe in the end it was all in vain. Perhaps the powerful talons had sunk deeper than he'd imagined, and the little boy was already dead from internal bleeding.

CHAPTER IV

In spite of Maria's proclamation that she would stand fast in the grass until Joe came to her, by the time he got home, she and a circle of neighbors and friends had moved into the house. When Joe's hurried strides crossed the threshold of the kitchen door and his arms reached for her, she began weeping again. Great drops of water spilled down his cheeks, too, and only gurgles came from his throat. Tear-stained people within the house backed away to allow husband and wife a private moment. Maria followed Joe's lead to their bedroom, and after he'd closed the door, he took her into his arms in a crushing embrace. Just the feel of him, the power in his arms, and the sturdines of his body gave her a new sense of strength. Her weeping petered out. She eased back and looked into her husband's glistening grey eyes.

"When they came to get you, did someone tell you all that happened?" she asked.

"Yeah. Couldn't believe it. Thought it was somebody's tall tale."

"A search party has already gone to the mountains, and they have a helicopter up there keeping the eagles away. Oh, God, Joe, do you think Joshua is still alive?"

"He's got to be. We can't think nothin' else. More men from the mine and from town are goin' up on the mountain. I got to go with them."

"Not just yet. Stay with me a while," she said, falling back into his arms. "You can't do anything they're not doing already. Just hold me."

He did, and momentarily, they both started weeping together. When they eased off and tried to get hold of themselves, she could see in his eyes that he hated himself

34

for losing emotional control. She could see his slow anger boiling up and he eased her back away from him.

"I still want to go. I'd like to climb that cliff, or that tree, or wherever that feathered bastard is hidin', and twist its neck from its body with my own bare hands."

"It was just a predator doing what its instincts told it to do," she tried to convince herself more than him.

"Before I could get out of the mine, the word spread quick and Spider Cornett came over to me. He said that just a few hours before he reported in for work, he'd been out to his farm and seen an eagle steal a lamb. He chased a second eagle away by shootin' at it, and now he thinks that he might have chased the eagle over here to our place. Feels real bad about it. Thinks he's responsible for the eagle stealin' Joshua."

"No reason for him to think that. He didn't know. And you'd think that the eagle would have gone to another farm and stolen a chicken or another lamb."

"Yeah. I know. I told him that, but he still feels pretty torn up about it. He's comin' with some of the others to do what he can up on the mountain."

Joe wiped his eyes dry. He seemed under full control now, but she still reached out to her dresser and picked up a bottle of pills.

"Dr. Smithers came by and insisted that I take these. I did, and it helps. Do you want one?"

She saw his eyes focus on the label that said Valium, and he shook his head.

"I don't need to be any zombie for what I've got to do. Honey, I want to get up on the mountain. . .do you understand?"

"Stay with me just a little while longer, and then you can go. Everybody has been so nice. Don't you think you ought to speak to some of the people here and thank them?"

"Yeah."

"Your mother's here, and you haven't even spoken to her. I almost gave her a heart attack. When I saw the eagle swoop down, I must have screamed and thrown the receiver into the sink. She heard my scream and heard the thud, and she said I was shrieking so loudly from the outside that she could still hear it in the receiver."

"I don't have to ask you if she made the twenty miles distance between us in record time. Lucky she didn't kill herself and two dozen more on the way," he said, and enjoyed one moment of lightness.

He started to step toward the door. She stopped him. She guided him to their bed, eased him down, took her place beside him. She slipped her arm around his muscular waist and again felt a wellspring of strength. She rested her cheek against his shoulder and said, "I can bear it better with you here, but I won't let myself believe that Joshua is dead."

In spite of the brave statement she began to break down again. For a moment, he said nothing, just sat there interlacing the fingers of his work-toughened hands.

In the silence she thought that she discerned a fatalistic acceptance in his expression, that perhaps he was already coming to terms with his son's probable death.

"Don't even think it, Joe," she said.

"How can I not think it when everything that's happened has happened?"

"Just don't think it, that's all."

"People have to face things. If the mine caves in, all my wishin' don't put the slate back in place and keep the tunnel clear. . ."

". . .this is different. Joshua's in God's hands."

"And the miners aren't in God's hands?"

"Oh, Joe, he's so little and frail. He's not a man. He can't fight for himself. . ."

He held her more tightly to him then, but she could sense that he wanted to say something but held it back as though uncertain.

"What?" she prompted.

"If Joshua is gone from us, we'll have another baby. I promise you that."

36

She jumped up, signalling the revulsion of even the thought.

"Joshua is alive! I've asked the Lord every second to protect him—bring him back to us."

"But if it don't turn out like that, can you remember that we've still got each other?"

She dropped down beside him, then, unable to let him go. His suggestion was unacceptable but even so, she let her vision sweep past him to their smooth bed that was overlaid with a family heirloom covering. Against her very will her mind considered anew. The bulging pillows began to represent their heads snuggled warmly beneath the covering. Their bed. For over five years, they had made passionate love, rotating the time of day, and sometimes doing so twice a day. Still, she had never become pregnant on her own. She'd even been desperate enough to try all of the old wives' tales about such matters. They had made love in the light of the moon, the dark of the moon, and at least a dozen times she had practically stood on her head to insure that not a single spermatozoa would be lost. But, of course, it had been her, not Joe.

"We'd better go on out, now," she finally said, refusing to entertain for another second the idea of starting over.

Wet eyes were everywhere visible, and Joe sought out his mother first and embraced her long and hard. Maria noticed that people were sneaking in food through the back door and that her counters and the breakfast table were almost fully covered. On the one hand, such loving kindness was appreciated, but on the other, it all suggested a wake.

Joe made the rounds within the living room, then moved out to the lawn where a large gathering still kept watch.

It was soon clear that a conspiracy was afoot. Someone began telling mildly comical stories, and momentum gathered until the welcome sound of banter was present. A couple of times, Maria found herself chuckling. But had she really, or was it just an illusion brought on by the Valium?

The mantle clock rang out six chimes. Maria needed no reminder that time was running out. The ominous tones reverberated throughout the room and brought in their echo of new fears. Several sets of eyes focused in her direction. Especially watchful over her were May Kernan, her fiftyish former boss, and Betty Lou Slade and Muffie Devlin, two of her former coworkers at the beauty shop. The three of them worked their way across the room to Maria's side. Predictably, May took charge.

"Can't we fix you and Joe a plate of food? A cup of coffee or hot tea? We feel so helpless," May said.

"I don't want anything to drink," Maria said, "but it would be nice if you fixed some for all the people outside. They must be getting tired just standing."

The three women hopped to the chore, and Maria looked after them with sisterly gratitude. May had begged her to come back to work, using the most outlandish flattery to accomplish her ends. But she and May had had an agreement on that score from her beginning: Maria had no intention of returning to work before Joshua was old enough for nursery school. Now, things might have changed. Five thousand, ten thousand, or thirty thousand dollars was a lot of money to raise. In truth, perhaps these three friends and coworkers were already thinking that. Funny how working together with them a sort of telepathic understanding of each other and a family-like closeness had developed. Sometimes they each claimed mind reading ability. And of all the training grounds in the world to quality one as a good amateur psychologist, a beauty shop certainly ranked high on the list.

Joe came back into the house and wedged his way between Maria and his mother.

"I can't hang around here any longer," he said to the both of them. "I don't know what's goin' on, and I've got to feel like I'm helpin' some way or another."

Maria realized that no word at all had been received

since the first search party had set off. She thought just as quickly that any kind of word just yet was a foolish expectation. After all, the deserted mountain range to which they journeyed offered no telephone booths, and the portable transmitters/receivers some of them carried might not have the range to reach back from the rugged mountains. But maybe television crews had gone to the mountains also and were somehow zooming back news with their more sophisticated equipment. She stepped to the T.V. set and flipped it on.

The local newscaster was relating the incident of Joshua's capture when the picture tube came to full brightness. Even so, he related no new developments, and as the segment began to end, the camera had come full focus on her. She hardly recognized the wild-looking woman whose eyes were mirrors of horror and whose body was visibly shaking. Yet, it was her, but for a moment she was able to make believe that this bad dream was the experience of someone else.

As the local news ended, Joe kissed her tenderly and with several of the other men took his leave.

The news and the continuing noise coming from the set had somehow established an atmosphere of normalcy. Not even Joe had made any wild new promises, nor bolstered her hopes with speculative assumptions. In Joe's void, though, periodically, new arms were about her waist or another cheek pressed to hers or a consoling voice said that everything would be all right. She felt it all and heard it all, but invariably her eyes would spill over and her doubts be reborn. Her mourning—and she had come to terms that it was specifically that—came in unexpected waves. For several minutes at a time, she could be in complete control, then without any warning whatsoever, her emotions would convulse, and she would have to go with the tide. Such reactions were reactions to death, not simple mother worry. Joshua was dead. Why couldn't she face that?

Through her peripheral vision, she was vaguely aware that the national newscaster's face had appeared on the television screen. She ignored him. Any other time, she would have been concerned about the woes of the world and which group of people, and where, had suffered today. Her own world seemed the only one important just now.

After a few minutes, however, her attention was spontaneous and rapt. She had caught the words Corbin, Kentucky, and the whole room had gotten quiet. She turned her full attention to the T.V. set and noticed in a way that she never had before how grim the TV anchorman's face could look, and how intensely his alert eyes glared back at her. She listened.

"The theft of an infant by an eagle is highly unusual, but today it happened in the small town of Corbin in eastern Kentucky," the newscaster continued. "Joshua Fremont, the only child of Maria and Joe Fremont, was stolen by a huge bird believed to be a golden eagle, from the lawn of the Fremont home. The child's mother had taken her infant to the out-of-doors for a sunbath, had gone back into her home to answer her telephone, and from the kitchen window had personally witnessed the theft of her three-weeks-old, 8½ pound, son. One witness who saw the eagle take flight with its prey stated that the talons of the eagle held the baby by the buttocks and upper shoulder area. It is thus believed that the child was not mortally wounded at the time and point of capture. The eagle was followed to its nest by a safety and rescue helicopter that was quickly dispatched in pursuit of the fleeing bird. The helicopter pilot was able to report the descent of the eagle into its nest with its booty intact. It is not known at this time whether the child is alive or dead."

Maria's mother-in-law moved to her side and held onto her. People from outside were streaming into the house now, but other than footsteps, the same solemn attentiveness prevailed. The newscaster continued:

"At this very hour, however, it is believed that a helicopter is hovering over the eagle's nest. It is thought that the downwash of the propeller blades will keep mature eagles from rending the infant's flesh as food for their young. No doubt this unusual human drama and heroic rescue effort will continue throughout the night.

Although the theft of small animals by eagles is commonplace throughout the world, the theft of an infant is extremely rare, but has happened a few times throughout the course of history. The most famous recorded incident of the theft of a baby by an eagle occurred at Rome in 63 B.C. That infant was none other than Caius Julius Caesar Octavianus, the Roman emperor more commonly known as Caesar Augustus. At the time, the infant and his mother—the sister of Julius Caesar—were guests on the lawn of the emperor's palace. The marauding eagle swept out of the sky, stole the child before the eyes of several onlookers, lifted the child above the treetops, circled the castle, and dropped the child essentially unharmed in the shrubbery of the palace grounds. Perhaps not surprisingly, the onlookers, and the Roman people themselves, looked upon this incident as a great and good omen. And so the child lived, and at the age of 18 became the heir—an adopted son—of Julius Caesar, and the master of the world in his own right at the age of 31. And as the eagle became the symbol of the mighty Roman Empire, so, too, did the great bird become emblematic of our own United States."

"It's a miracle! It's a miracle!" Sadie Chambers' shrill voice split the air. "Little Joshua is anointed!"

As startling as the outburst was, Sadie Chambers and her brand of religion were not unknown to most of Corbin. She claimed the ability to speak in tongues and to interpret when others spoke in the same heavenly language. She was a leader in her charismatic church and a woman known for her benevolence to all and a willing martyr to her faith.

As the woman ranted on and lifted her extended arms and hands to heaven, thus making herself the receptacle of more divine wisdom, a few of the older men and women present went to her with calming voices and restraining caresses. Sadie would not be calmed, and she came and knelt before Maria.

"Joshua is alive," Sadie cooed. "Didn't you hear the newsman? Didn't you hear him tell how Caesar Augustus was lifted by the eagle as a sign of his anointing? So it is with your child! Joshua has been commissioned for the Lord's work. I see! I know! Joshua is alive!"

With tender gentleness, an old man and an old woman whom Maria hardly knew led Sadie from the room into the out-of-doors. Even thus removed, her sudden transition into speaking in tongues could be heard through the screen door over the newscaster's voice. The incident unnerved Maria for reasons that she could not explain. She and Joe were Methodists, and the charismatic faith was not something either of them had experienced personally.

Even so, for a moment she allowed herself to believe the prophecy. But far beyond the prophecy, she felt an uplifting moment, the result of Sadie Chambers' proclamation. The woman had spoken with such conviction, such intonations of truth. Maria had to force such thoughts from her. She could not allow herself the luxury of believing specualtion, no matter how well intended. She forced her attention back to the newscaster.

"There is an especial reason why the abduction of Joshua Fremont is an unusual loss for the citizens of Corbin. The child's parents, Maria and Joe Fremont, were the recipients of an outpouring of community help in an unusual way. Maria, a beautician, and Joe, an electrician in the local coal mine, were unable to have a child. When it was discovered that Maria could give birth only by the in vitro fertilization process, and the family was unable to come up with the money needed for the expensive process on their own, the community at large pitched in and raised the necessary funds. When the first in vitro fertilization attempt failed, the community again put its shoulder to the wheel and had a second fund raising, after which Maria enjoyed a healthy and successful pregnancy. It was thus that an entire community became surrogate parents, and the heart of all America goes out to the people of Corbin tonight."

Heavy footsteps came through the back door and paused behind Maria's chair. A cool hand rested on her cheek, and she turned to see the wet eyes of her and Joe's aging minister. He bent low and pressed his cheek to hers.

"I got back to town as quickly as I could. I heard about it on my car radio. Might we pray?"

"Let's do it here. Here where we're all together," Maria said.

The prayer was long, passionate, and uplifting. Afterwards, people began to drift away. She could wish that all of her friends and neighbors—and even the near strangers who felt a need to offer their support by their presence—could all stay with her and stand vigil during the long night to come.

The emptier the house became, the closer May, Betty Lou, and Muffie stuck with her. May whispered into Maria's ear, "You need some personal attention. You'd best go to your room and change."

Betty Lou's eyes were focused on Maria's chest area also. Betty Lou was a mother of three and still under 22 years old. Maria looked down at herself. In the artificial calm her pills had wrought, the moving tribute that the newscaster had paid to her child and her community, and the sense of peace her friends and neighbors and her minister had brought to her, Maria was not even conscious that her nipples had leaked milk until her bra and her blouse were wet from the spillage. Somehow, on this occasion, she was beyond embarrassment, but a different kind of realization registered upon her senses. It was past supper time, and her precious baby would be puckering his lips and nuzzling only to find nothing but sticks and grass. A new wave of mourning assaulted her body, and deep sobs escaped her throat.

"And, it'll get cold tonight." Maria cried between sobs. "What if it frosts?"

Muffie took her friend in her arms and said, "He'll be all right. That hovering helicopter is not going to leave him. The copter will keep the air so stirred up that there's no way it can frost. Besides, I'll bet my Jeep on the fact that that copter is overheating right now like crazy. Why, the heat off that churning engine will radiate out and keep Joshua as warm as toast."

Maria wanted to believe it, and to a degree she could. Muffie, as small and delicate as she was, knew about engines and choppers and things like that. She even did some of the mechanical work on her own vehicle as a kind of avocation.

The longing for Joshua soon became unbearable again, and between hugs and well wishes of still more departing friends and neighbors, Maria began to pace.

"Do you think we'll be hearing anything before midnight?" she asked no one in particular.

"It depends on how tough it is getting to the top of that mountain," a male member of her church intoned.

"They can't even lower the basket of a rescue helicopter until daylight," someone else opined. "It'd be too dangerous to try anything in the dark with the wind whirlin' round you and scrubby trees stickin' out of the rocks in all directions."

Such responses, truthful as they were, brought a chill to the room. But dozens of men were scaling the mountain now at this very moment. She hoped the first thing that they would hear on reaching the pinnacle was an infant's cry.

CHAPTER V

Much to the surprise of Dowless and his fellow volunteers, they were able to get a little deeper into the mountain than first supposed. By the use of a deserted log road, they estimated being only six to eight miles removed from the mountain peak.

Having crossed county lines—from Knox into Whitley—they had observed protocol and invited the participation of Whitley county Sheriff Otto Stanford. Stanford and one of his deputies rendezvoused with Dowless and his Corbin forces. Representing the Knox County Sheriff's Office was Deputy Sheriff Boyd Groves. Stanford looked young for a county sheriff, and Dowless guessed his age at not more than thirty years. He was clearly an eager beaver and anxious to get on with the challenge.

Groves, on the other hand, was an older vet in law enforcement. The two professionals already knew each other well, having worked together on crimes of overlapping interest.

Of Stanford's deputy, it was decided that he would be permanently stationed at the intersection of the log road and the unpaved county road. He could thus point late arriving volunteers in the right direction and serve also as a communications link back to town. Although Dowless realized they'd be high on the mountain peak, they might require radio relay at critical moments.

The little band was comprised of twenty-three men now, and there was less than ninety minutes of daylight left. A few of the men had equipped themselves with flashlights, lanterns, rope, axes, and other utilitarian supplies. The upward journey was clearly to be a case of plowing through the jungle, and the darkness of night would be a monumental hindrance.

When the walking got a little better, Otto Stanford moved up to Dowless' side and posed a few questions. Stanford had been brought up-to-date by his counterpart from Corbin, but he disagreed with everybody that there was any possible chance for the baby's survival.

"We've got to save that child," Dowless insisted. "The baby belongs to the whole town. We can expect a lynchin' if we come back empty handed."

"Then if that's the way it is, consider yourself in command," Stanford said. "You've been on top of it from the beginning, so take the ball and run with it."

Upon reaching a plateau that was exceedingly dense with small hemlock trees, they all stopped for a breather. The aroma of the hemlocks and the purity of the mountain air were like putting on a mask and breathing pure, scented oxygen. Dowless found a tall boulder and stood upon it. When he'd made radio contact with the chopper, he could tell by Loopy's voice that he was growing weary.

"Seen anything of that National Guard chopper, yet?" Dowless asked.

"No, but I can tell you right now, he'd better not waste any more time. You could fry an egg on the engine of this machine, and the fuel indicator has only a hairline to go before hittin' the red zone."

"Not to mention that the pilot could use a little fuel of his own," Dowless reached for a moment of mirth. "You may have to come down. I'm not goin' to have you endanger your life, and havin' you drop into the trees like a rock off the moon would be a double fatality."

"I'm off to the side a little bit now. The eagle's nest is in the top of a partially dead tree, and a column of rock comes up under the lesser fork of the tree and supports it. It's too shadowy now to see anything, but a little earlier, I could swear I saw the baby kick his legs."

"I hope you're not seein' things," Dowless said with a lump in his throat. "It's already gettin' chilly down here, and before dawn it'll be ten degrees colder up there."

46

"Don't worry about frost settlin' on his pink little nose. I'm sendin' down heat like a blower and keepin' the wind churned like whipped cream."

"But you're discountin' one thing: if the mountain winds run high tonight, they'll sweep engine heat away and freeze everything beneath."

There was a long period of silence as Loopy considered. When he did come back on, he said, "We can't let that happen. You guys have got to get here on the double. Can't you make it from where you are in a couple of hours—"

"No way," Dowless said. "Two or three miles an hour goin' straight up is the best we can hope for. Even so, we're goin' to be an exhausted bunch when we get there. Some of these guys are young bucks, but others like myself are headed for the half century mark."

"There's one thing I can do for you as long as I'm up here," Loopy said. "When you come into view, I can give you some directions. It'll soon be dark, but if you can shine some light skyward, I'll be able to spot you."

"Good idea. What we really need is a couple dozen pack mules."

Again, there was a moment of noncommunication, but finally Loopy said, "You're sure that National Guard helicopter is on the way?"

"The state police confirmed it before we hit the trail."

"Where's it comin' from?"

"I don't know," Dowless confessed. "Louisville. Lexington. Maybe from Paducah for all I know. He'll be lookin' for you and I'm sure the pilot will make radio contact when he gets closer in. You sure you're all right? Set it down if you have to to save your own life. . ."

". . .no way," Loopy barked. "I'm not worried about me, but what happens if my fuel supply runs out and the NG chopper hasn't got here? I'll have to set down for fuel, and then who watches the baby?"

"When that time comes, you've got no choice. It won't prove a thing to lose you and your chopper as well. Besides, if you fell to earth in that high, dry timber, you'd

47

start a huge bonfire. Come down if you have to. We'll just have to take the chance. Maybe the mature eagles wouldn't move in at night anyway."

"Don't count on it," Loopy said. "To eagles, the crown of this mountain under moonlight may be like daylight to us."

"I'm signin' off now," Dowless said. "Let me know the second you see or hear of any help comin'. You listen to me, now, and no heroics up there. Hear?"

"I hear ya. Over an out."

Otto Stanford and a few of the others had gathered around Dowless and had heard the last part of the transmission.

"How long before we're in trouble up there?" Stanford asked.

"Not long," Dowless answered. "The chopper's over-heatin'; must have sucked some leaves into the intake, and it's doubtful that he's got another half hour's worth of fuel left. Why don't you ring your deputy up down at the crossroads and have him find out from the KSP if there's been any delay with the NG chopper since we last communicated?"

Stanford replaced Dowless upon the rock and started his own communication. Dowless sat down on the trunk of a fallen tree and caught his breath. He was already tired, and there was a long way to go. The realization hit him of just how out of shape he really was. As busy and active as he always had been, it was obviously not the type of exercise that prepared one for mountain climbing. And, too, he mentally confessed that there was still a lot of beer floating around between his hide and his bone. At 48, he was not a bad physical specimen, but the belly blubber had pushed him up to 190 lbs., and that was excessive bulk on a 5 foot 8 inch frame. He took a red bandana handkerchief from his hip pocket and wiped his face. Moisture oozed from the cup-sized bald spot at the crown of his head and dribbled down his neck hair and down his back. At 18, he had married Mabel when she was only 16, and six children in a row had been born to them to feed and clothe. Those children were all on their own at last, and four of them, college graduates. He and Mabel were grandparents five times over, now, and maybe that fact made the life of Joshua Fremont seem all the more precious. And, too, he had a special interest in Joshua Freemont just like so many other people of Corbin did. He had invested $350 in that miracle child.

"The NG chopper is definitely on the way," Otto Stanford interrupted Dowless' reverie.

They were off again, but it was not long before Dowless and Knox County Deputy Boyd Groves were falling behind.

"You think they're tyring to tell us something?" Groves chuckled. "I've got a good urge to apply for the dispatcher's job next year."

Dowless looked over at Groves and took note of his slender build, but even before Groves confessed it, Dowless could tell by the other man's breathing that he was probably a heavy smoker.

Daylight faded still further, and they began to encounter vast limestone outcroppings. At a couple of points, they had to backtrack and find a routing around the forbidding stone walls. Once around and on top, they could see the distance of their progress and were thus encouraged.

Dowless' radio unexpectedly crackled to life, and the intruding voice echoed against the stone walls.

"I've just had contact," Loopy reported excitedly, "and I can see the NG chopper approachin' from the west."

"Bingo!" Dowless responded. "As quickly as they arrive on the scene and you can give them a rundown, I want you out of here. Go home, get some beans, and sack out. You've earned it."

"Let's hope I've got fuel enough to get back to base. After I tune them in to your frequency, you can give the background details while I head for home."

"Roger," Dowless confirmed.

Dowless announced the good news in the loudest voice that he could muster. There was an immediate round of cheers.

Within five minutes, they could hear but not see the arrival of the NG chopper. The very sound of the big machine engendered confidence and suggested awesome power. In a couple of minutes more, they saw the Hughes swing off to the north. As Loopy passed overhead, he chimed in with an "Adios and good hunting!" farewell and headed in the direction of Corbin.

As the rescue entourage gained new heights, a commanding voice came over the air waves.

"This is Captain Slater. Who's in charge down there?"

"I guess I've been elected." Dowless said and identified himself more properly. "We've got one sheriff and deputy, plus a smatterin' of volunteers. More are on the way. Thanks for comin', and now I'll give you a complete update."

"Looks like we didn't get here any too soon," Captain Slater said. "That Hughes was throwing out vapor from overheating. What's your battle plan?"

Dowless first made sure that the chopper commander had the complete picture and was aware of all the obstacles as he saw them. It was dark for real, now, and a number of the rescuers already had their flashlights and lanterns snapped on.

"How far up the mountain are you?" Captain Slater inquired.

"Maybe a fourth of the way up. When we get out from under another limestone shelf dead ahead, you ought to be able to see our flashlight beams."

"There's still a little light here on the peak," Captain Slater said, "so I suggest that we proceed with a rescue operation. Besides, we've got underbelly spotlights to aid us. I see no reason why we can't lower the basket and at least make a trial run."

"Negative," Dowless insisted. "Since there's no immediate danger to the child, I think it would be wiser if you wait until we get there. That way, one or two of us can climb the nest tree, and if you guys bump target and dislodge things, we can catch the fallout. At the very least, we can help direct you from below. I don't have to remind you that this isn't a pilot lost at sea—it's 8½ pounds of infant flesh."

"What makes you think it's alive? Your Hughes pilot said he hadn't seen any movement in the nest for over an hour."

"Faith. The child's alive. We're going under that assumption. Are we agreed on that? Nobody takes any chances that would be in conflict with that—right?"

"Roger. Do you object if we begin some practice maneuvers?"

Dowless called Otto Stanford, Boyd Groves, and three other rescue leaders over for a conference. It was lengthy enough that Captain Slater's voice had gathered an edge.

"Do you read me down there? We want to do a couple of practice maneuvers."

"Roger. But I don't have to tell you that keepin' mature eagles away from the nest and keepin' the air stirred up and warm is the first priority," Dowless insisted.

"We've no trouble in churning up the air for a quarter of a mile," Captain Slater's voice had an even more annoyed tone to it. "As for warmth generated beneath us, we could heat a fair sized barn. It's also my opinion that mature eagles will not move about at night."

"You're probably dead on about the eagles and night-time, but if that feathered parent is as sharp as I think it is, it'll be worried about feedin' its young. I just hope those baby eagles haven't started fixin' suppers for themselves."

Captain Slater's voice was slow in replying as though he needed to digest what Dowless had said.

"How long can that little boy hold out without milk—or water? I'm not even close to being a papa yet," Slater said.

"Probably two or three days or more, but I hope to God that doesn't have any bearin'."

"Roger. We'll be keeping an eye out for your lights. Over and out."

By eight-forty, Dowless believed they had reached the half-way point of the mountain. The lights of the communities of Barbourville and Heidrick shown brightly in the distance. Although he was now puffing like a freight train, the view and height itself was exhilarating. Memories. He and Mabel had gone on their brief honeymoon to Gatlinburg in the neighboring state of Tennessee. On that occasion, they had hiked high into the Great Smoky Mountains where earth truly met heaven. He had even attempted to make love to her there, on the most aromatic of leaf beds. A grove of white pines had sheltered them, but in spite of the little bit of Eden they had found for themselves, they'd been interrupted by bear cubs who in turn were pursued by a very angry mother. He chuckled to himself at the remembrance. It now seemed a thousand years ago.

"Slater to ground rescue. We see your lights. If terrain allows it, hold fifteen degrees to your north. You're going off course."

"Roger. Thanks for the assist. Too bad you can't swing down the mountain and pick us old men up in that basket."

"Tough luck. We'd better stay on station. The temperature is dropping up here. By midnight, frost crystals will be decorating the trees and stone ledges."

"How's the wind factor up there?" Dowless asked.

"Rising faster than we thought," Slater confessed. "We did a couple of practice maneuvers, and we've already got enough wind draft to swing the basket twenty degrees off of true vertical."

"Then you're tellin' me that a rescue attempt from the chopper is as dangerous as hell. If there's that much wind and more to come, the swingin' basket with a man in it could well dislodge the baby, nest and all. Either that, or the bouncin' might snap tree limbs and send them like spears directly into the eagle's nest."

"We're not inexperienced at this," Slater said, the tinge of annoyance back in his voice.

"No offense meant, but I'm thinkin' about you boys, too. You get that basket and hoist cable hooked around one of those craggy trees just right, and you may find yourself in trouble."

"We've been in worse fixes," Slater said confidently.

Dowless was happy for the show of confidence. There was much to be said for the cockiness of youth. He was glad that middle-aged men didn't have to fight wars or else none would ever be won.

Unexpectedly, Dowless had an inspiration.

"Why can't you guys get down a little closer to the nest for a moment and see if you can focus one of your spotlights on target? Sure would give us guys a shot in the arm if you could report that the baby is playin' with his toes."

"We've already tried it. The stiff breeze up here is blowing the limb of an adjacent tree across the path of light. We'll keep trying," Slater promised, "but we'll just have to wait until the wind takes a breather. Over and out."

Dowless pocketed his radio, and the light jacket he had brought along had begun to feel good.

At nine-twenty, one of the hikers flushed a skunk. Its odiforous presence settled upon them all like a fog.

"What kind of friggin' animal would want to live this high up?" Boyd Groves grumbled.

"You don't know the half of it," Otto Stanford chimed in. "My uncle was sheriff of this county before me, and he and his deputies, along with state and federal men, flushed two families of moonshiners from between these rocks. I think there's a flush spring in the next plateau we hit which they probably used as a water supply."

"Right now, a little snort might be what the doctors ordered," Dowless said. "My knees and hip joints could do with a little bit of numbin'."

"Not to mention that upliftin' feelin' that comes with just one little glassful," Groves added with a chuckle.

"Say—if there were shiners operatin' up here, maybe we can find their pathway and have it a little easier," Dowless said.

"Small chance," Stanford countered. "You could look for their path for a week and not find it. They're geniuses at covering their tracks."

Conversation was difficult while puffing and walking, and Dowless let the banter peter out. It was mostly the younger men who were breaking trail, but some of them, too, were showing signs of fatigue.

"Slater to ground rescue," the radio spluttered to life. "We finally got a light on the eagle's nest. I just got a look through binoculars, and the infant is either asleep or dead. I could see one baby eagle clearly and a shadowy area that may represent a second or third bird."

Dowless swallowed hard but said nothing. He focused his flashlight into the faces of Stanford, Groves, and a couple of the other men walking nearest to him. Each of them in turn lowered his vision to the ground at his feet.

CHAPTER VI

Deep inside a yawning cave whose mouth resembled the rough outline of the letter "M," Necco Tufarelli slowly emerged from a drug induced sleep. As reeling as his senses now were, he could have sworn that continuous thunder had been resounding against the cave walls for a long time, or else new and different hallucinations had come upon him. He stretched and stood up on the Army blanket that separated his body from the dirt of the cave floor. The faintly rumbling, grinding sound could still be heard, and when he walked a few paces and placed his hands on the cave wall, there was some kind of vibration or sensory transmission. Any new phenomenon frightened him. Since returning from Nam, he had walked up the southwest face of the mountain, and after exploring it from every side, had found his present haven of rest. On a clear day, he could almost see the front door of his boyhood home in the little community of Rockholds just beyond the foothills. There was nothing for him anywhere. He had repudiated civilization, and if he never saw a city or a town or even another human being, he would feel no sense of loss.

In spite of his wishes, practicality demanded some compromise. At least twice a month he had to walk back down the mountain to collect his government disability check at the post office, and buy food and supplies. Getting a supply of drugs in Rockholds was another matter. For a brief time, he'd had a supplier, but the long arm of the law had done away with that source. Now, his supplies of white powder, hash, and marijuana required a bus trip to the larger towns of Corbin and London some miles to the north.

He attempted some bends and in-place exercises, but

he was still stiff and wobbly. The exercise was making him sick in his stomach and he gave it up. During his fitful sleep, he had evidently slid off of the blanket into the dirt, and he brushed the residue from the Army fatigue trousers that were his daily uniform. There was no patriotism left in him, God knew, but that wasn't the point. The fact was that he didn't have but a couple of outfits of civilian clothes, and he saved those for his bus trips. He finally sat down on a shelf of rock and pulled on his combat boots.

Was it his hallucinating imagination again, or did his very ass itch from some kind of vibration? He wanted to go outside, but right now he didn't trust himself. He was always seeing things that were not there and missing things that he suspected *were* there. But that was the hell of it. He never knew for sure anymore. Everything was like the day he'd walked south down over the mountain from the cave's mouth to the trickle of water that supplied his needs. As he had filled his canteen and his bucket, a water lizard had flowed into the larger vessel while it was filling. Ever since he'd been a boy, he'd caught lizards for fish bait. He also knew that lizards always headed for the bottom of any container in which they found themselves. But the damnable creature that had been accidentally imprisoned in his water bucket swam for the top and pucked a bubble right in Necco's face. Something crazy was going on. That fuggin' lizard should have stayed at the bottom with his mouth shut. In some way or another, the creature was thumbing his nose, and Necco knew it. That had happened yesterday, and he didn't know why it bothered him so much. Things like that would grab hold of him and not let go for days and sometimes weeks. He tried again to shake the thought and feeling, and when he couldn't he kicked at a piece of protruding shale sticking from the cave wall. With the full force of his boot, he snapped it like an icicle. Flying shards ricochetted against the globe of the miner's lantern that he used for illumination.

Even though the cave interior was dimly lit, he could

see the form of something crossing his blanket. He reached for it. Examining his captive nearer to the light, he saw that it was a huge and hairy spider. He turned the insect in his hand until its beady eyes faced his own. He held its grape-shaped body between his thumb and forefinger and stripped away one hairy leg at a time. When it was legless, he squeezed thumb and forefinger very gradually. As though an egg had been crushed, slimy residue ran down his thumb and forefinger into the palm of his hand. He'd been dead wrong. He had guessed that the eyes would have popped first. Wrong or not, the act made him feel good.

His imagination—even in lucid moments—was fragile and unpredictable. Around him, people did not act right. People were strange, period. The hell with them. That's the reason he had searched and found his new home within the rocks. But there were days on end when he missed them and would find himself weeping. At times like that there were two of him. One wanted to go home, and the other wanted to flee from humanity. But where was home? His great-great-parental grandfather had come from Italy to the coal town of Jenkins, and was known as a Wop. His grandfather also had been heir to that derisive and stupid prejudice. There were still people in Whitley county who hadn't the sense to know that the term only meant "without passports." He—Necco—never knew whether that dehumanizing tag was an element in his father's downfall, or whether he just couldn't take one more day in the mines, and had surrendered himself to the bottle. In any event, his so called home—not a great deal better than the miner's shacks of yesteryear—lay in the plain below, occupied by a man in a constant alcoholic stupor, and by a woman long devoid of any hope. Wops. All of them were still only a bunch of Wops. Time itself had helped them to blend well into the mixing bowl of humanity as found in Eastern Kentucky. Nobody would believe it now, but there had been a time at the turn of the century when Slavs, Italians, Germans, blacks, and a host from other countries had invaded the coal fields like a hungry army. They had come to Appalachia truly believing they'd be the inheritors of new wealth and new freedom in the land of black diamonds. Many if not most had descended into torment, and it was a hell into which subsequent generations would also be condemned.

A deepening depression settled on Necco. At the worst of times, there was the taste of metal and corn meal in his mouth. He couldn't begin to explain why that particular taste eddied up out of his gut, but it was as distinct as a mouthful of ball bearings over-sprinkled with corn meal rolling around on his tongue. He rolled a joint and smoked it rapidly. Afterwards, he rolled another and inhaled it with considerably more leisure. His mind started to float, but he could still feel that damnable vibration against the soles of his feet when he paced, or caused his ass to itch when he sat down on a ledge. Even in drugged euphoria, he knew that he was not imagining the vibrations. Maybe the mountain was getting ready to blow its stack. Ash and hot lava would bury him in his sepulcher, and nobody would know the difference or even give a damn. Maybe he ought to break off the next of the shale ledge and fashion his own tombstone. The thought almost made him laugh, but the attempt was hollow and ended with a kind of desperate cry. On the tombstone he would inscribe, "*Here lies Necco Tufarelli, a good ole boy. Birthed in the mountains and baptised in coal dust. He hoped and dreamed and went to war and found a new kind of hell in Vietnam.*"

He lost count of how many joints he'd smoked, but he was really spaced out now. He needed a breath of fresh air, got up, and walked toward the cave's entrance. Beyond the opening he could see that moonlight bathed the out-of-doors in a silver glow. But wait. He could feel the vibrations on the soles of his feet stronger than ever now. Before he stepped outside, the feeling got stronger, and now he could hear the thundering noise that accompanied the vibrations. Once out in the moonlight, he recognized that sound. He'd know that thundering anywhere. He started to shake violently, and for the life of him he couldn't move. When his legs would obey him, he circled the ledge and climbed out on top of the limestone shelf that gave formation to his primitive abode. Then he saw it. It was a chopper and a big one. That silhouette and that sound were as burned in his mind as a brand into cattle flesh. The fearful-looking machine hovered at the peak of the mountain, its side-mounted red and green warning lights flashing like the eyes of a space monster.

He ran, stumbled and fell, picked himself up, and ran again. They were coming for him. They wanted him back, but he'd never go. He ran back into the cave to hide himself. He was trembling so violently that he tried four times to roll another joint before he could steady his fingers enough to do it. He tried to reason things out, but his mind was as jumbled as a short-circuited computer. Maybe the mountain top was a drug drop site, and the chopper was only completing some kind of relay delivery. Or maybe it was a pickup point for illicitly made whiskey. But no, his mind was playing tricks on him, or he was playing tricks on his mind; he didn't know which. That chopper had military markings on it. It was too well outlined against the clear sky and illuminated enough by the bright moon that there was no doubt. They had come for him. They wanted to take him back to the Mekong again where he had once waded neck deep in slimy swamps to search out an enemy who was never seen but always there, somewhere in the shadows. Hell, no. He wouldn't go. He had gone and paid a terrible price, once. Part of him was still there. Another part of him had been left at the military hospital in Saigon. Eight months—or so he had been told—had been spent there, and yet to this day he couldn't remember a single week of the confinement prior to fifteen days before his discharge.

He threw the butt down and ground it out with his heel. He grabbed the lantern and headed for the rear of the cave. There, in his cache of weaponry, he strapped on a cartridge belt and stuffed a 45 automatic in the holster. He slung a M-16 rifle across one shoulder and a Browning automatic rifle across the other. The pockets of his fatigue jacket and trousers were filled with extra clips of ammunition, and just in case, he strapped on a hunting knife. He began to feel good again. The powerful firearms seemed not to laden him down but to generate waves of elation. He even liked the smell of the gun metal. So he did have in his possession this illegal military hardware. So what? Anybody could buy them on the black market, and it was the best expenditure of his mustering-out pay that he could have made. Deep down, he knew that sooner or later They would come for him. He hadn't know how or when, but there were avenues in his battered mind that were still capable of cunning and self preservation. Tonight, that mystery had been resolved; someone knew the hermit's hiding place, had reported it, and now the military chopper had come for him. Two opposing forces could play at that game. He snuffed out the light. He wouldn't need it. The night was clear; the moon was bright. Besides, the old know-how began to come back. He had fought many a firefight in the bleakness of night with the added horror of monsoon rains pouring down. He remembered it more clearly now. His instincts began to sharpen, and it would not be long before his eyes had the sharpness of an eagle's.

Ascending the west face of the mountain, Necco could feel the earth and stone seemingly vibrate with greater intensity. The whirling blades of that hovering Huey chopper spoke of awesome power. He had not remembered the sounds of the engine being so loud, but now the thundering sounds were ricochetting off the rocks like machine gun bullets. If one could dismiss the fearful silhouette for a moment, there was a degree of cheer in seeing the blinking warning lights. Even so, he could only get momentary glimpses of the craft. As he walked ever upward, trees and craggy cliffs blocked his view.

Although the climb was a steeper and steeper incline, he felt no fatigue. On the contrary, some unholy surge of adrenalin was giving him power beyond himself. In another hundred yards, it was impossible to stand and walk, and thus he found himself using all fours to gain the pinnacle.

With sixty or seventy yards more to go, he passed under a ledge overhang and lost sight of the aircraft. Maybe the pilot had veered off and sought a flatter place for landing a little further north along the mountain peak. But maybe they were playing cat and mouse with him. Undoubtedly, they had infrared night scopes aboard. They could see a man or an animal—or a machine—moving in the darkness. Maybe they had already spotted him. They would land and send a squad for him.

When he had cleared the rock ledge, he saw quickly that the chopper had moved very little. What he saw next sent shock waves the length of his spine. Belly lights had come on, and the helicopter's rescue basket was descending. Maybe that meant that the squad was already on the ground encircling him, and that he would be the one to be tied into the basket and retrieved like some helpless hooked fish.

He wasted no time. Using a tree limb as a tripod, he aimed the M-16 and brought it to life with short bursts of fire. It was either an echo or he could hear the slugs slam into the side and belly of the chopper. Even so, nothing seemed to be happening, and he reached for the Browning automatic and aimed for the nose. The bark of the deadly weapon obliterated the engine noise, and for a brief glorious moment Necco knew that he alone commanded the mountainside. He swung the muzzle of the Browning automatic slowly until the spitting bullets had swept along the top of the fuselage. Maybe some of the projectiles would hit the rotor shaft or the blades themselves.

He put a new clip in the M-16 and held a bead directly on the rotor shaft. He worked it up and down like shooting into the trunk of a tree, and before he'd expended the clip, he heard the chopper engine seem to increase speed. A piece of wood or metal or something came sailing into the trees not twenty yards in front of him. The chopper soon began to shimmy like a belly dancer, and against the skyline, he could see puffs of smoke exiting the nose section. In a matter of seconds, the chopper was veering off, out of control, down the southeast section of the mountain.

He had won. Necco Tufarelli had won. They were not taking him back. Never again. His victory, his overwhelming elation, were mind blowing. Here he stood, king of the mountain, still a free man, free for his wounds to heal amidst the perfumed sanctity of nature.

But wait. Was a squad of soldiers closing in on him? Even without the chopper, they could march him handcuffed and defenseless down the mountain face by force. That would be the ultimate humiliation—that he should be marched a prisoner through the streets of his own community. But maybe it would be just as when he'd come home. Save for a handful, no one seemed to know or care that he, nor any of the other veterans, had done a job and made it back.

He waited and listened. Not a sound from any quarter. He began to move cautiously and to close the distance to the mountain peak where he would have a better view and a better tactical advantage.

The next sound he heard could only be his mind and his ears playing tricks on him. He heard it again, and he tried to deny the sound as resolutely as he daily denied his own diminishing sanity. Yet, there it was again. An infant's cry. But no, it couldn't be. Maybe it was a panther or some other cat's mating call. Maybe the chopper had frightened the entire animal kingdom into fearful cries. He shouldered the M-16 again and aimed; waited. The sound ceased for two or three minutes, and then it came again. Cautiously, he moved in the direction of the sound. The piteous wail was like a beacon, guiding his footsteps. As he came closer, he looked against the skyline and saw an eagle's nest lodged between a scraggly tree and a column of rock. He lowered the M-16. It was from there that the baby's cries were originating.

He let his weapons slide from his shoulders. He emptied his pockets of ammunition and looked again to the large nest against the moon-bright sky.

The tree was made for climbing. Its jagged limbs stuck out right and left like the treads of a ladder. As he ascended the tree, the infant tuned up again. Maybe it had the sense to know someone was coming.

At the treetop, as though he had not believed his own ears, he reached into the nest. His hand found the leg of a very small baby. Surprisingly, his single touch effected a calming of the frantic outcries. Something suddenly pecked at his hand, and he drew his arm away quickly. He could have reasoned that it was baby eagles. But one of the birds was cold and still. He could feel that its head had been lodged under the baby's leg. Undoubtedly, the child had smothered it without ever knowing the difference.

He buttoned his fatigue jacket halfway up his chest. The only way he could carry the child to earth safely was to stuff it down the opening of his jacket, button the jacket most of the way up, then hold a supporting arm underneath the buttocks of the infant.

He did all this with great joy, now. Of course his mind had not been playing tricks on him. As he cradled the infant against his chest, his glistening eyes sought out a particular star. He was not only sure that everything happening was real, but now he also knew why this child had been so miraculously delivered to him.

CHAPTER VII

On the other side of the mountain, Dowless, Sheriff Stanford, Deputy Groves, and their fellow rescue workers stood silently in stupified wonder. Only minutes before, Captain Slater's urgent voice had come over the radio saying, "What's going on down there? We're taking on small arms fire!"

"It sure as thunder isn't us!" Dowless had almost screamed into the instrument.

"Are you sure there's not clans of moonshiners operating up in these mountains?"

Dowless hadn't even answered. He was listening to see if he could hear rifle fire, but the noise of the chopper, as the rescuers had drawn closer to the mountaintop, obliterated any other sounds. Then, when Dowless had formulated an answer, it was too late. Either the chopper radio was dead, or Slater himself was disabled. In any event, in seconds more, the chopper was wobbling wildly out of control down the mountain face. Dowless had not been able to see where the disabled chopper came to earth, but he had heard tree limbs breaking, which implied that the aircraft's descent might have been softened by coming down amid groves of pine and hemlock trees. There had finally been the sound of a dull thud, but thank God, there had been no explosion. Fearful that there might be an orange ball of flame emerging from the craft at any moment—with wounded men most likely trapped inside—Dowless sent half of his volunteers back down the mountain. The deputy on radio relay and directions duty would no doubt be the first one on the scene, and he could handle the call for ambulance assistance as well. No doubt also, a second and perhaps a third rescue team would be on the way up the mountain by now. He tried without success to reach the hoped-for newcomers on the radio. Maybe some of them would turn back and lend assistance.

Dowless got his diminished forces moving forward again, and nobody had to remind another that any further delay might be fatal. Now, the little boy, if he was alive, stood literally naked to the entire bird and animal kingdom. The moon was bright enough, Dowless suspected, that the mother eagle would attempt to return.

In spite of himself, Dowless hesitated occasionally and looked to his rear. He noticed Standford and Groves doing the same thing.

"You think what I'm thinking?" Stanford finally ventured.

"Yeah," Dowless answered. "All we need to see now is a delayed explosion of that downed chopper, and those pine groves will go up like torches."

"Not to mention that as dry as the ground is, we'll have a forest fire racing up the mountain. Then where would we be?" Groves added.

Dowless shivered at the thought. If such a thing happened, they would be trapped if the fire moved in a rage and spread rapidly. He hadn't taken special note of it before, but now as they moved off again, he noticed here and there the large accumulation of dry winter leaves.

His light beam and the beams of others stabbed into the darkness. Dowless envisioned a hundred phantom forms, and suddenly it was so deathly quiet. Now, they had no beacon above the pinnacle to lead them in, to literally point them to the eagle's nest. Nevertheless, with the aid of the helicopter floods and the clarity of the mountaintop against the skyline, they had already picked out certain landmarks. They would find the child. They had to find the child. Even if little Joshua were already dead, tragedy would be added to tragedy if his little body were shredded or picked to pieces.

The going got rougher. The dirt and leaves played out the closer they got to the pinnacle. Sharp rock ledges ripped through the trousers into the flesh of the advance men, and after this treacherous terrain was bypassed, they encountered rock face so wind and rain polished that footing was nearly impossible to gain.

Terry Binns—the youngest man in the group—reached the top first. His silhouette against the skyline made him look twenty four feet tall rather than the quarter of that, his actual size.

"Corbin is lit up like a Christmas tree," Terry announced his own arrival. "And I can see London and Mount Vernon—purt near to Somerset and Manchester. Man, wouldn't I like to have an A-frame or a log house sittin' up here."

"I hear you don't even have a girl friend any more," Groves jibed.

There was a round of laughter. Everybody in Corbin knew everybody else, and a good part of the time everybody knew everybody else's business.

"Yeah, but if I could get Betty up on this mountain with the wind whippin' her hair, and me with my arms looped around her, I could get her to agree to anything," Terry retorted.

There was a round of guffaws as if all those present from Corbin well knew that Betty was already long gone or comfortable in the arms of another. Dowless said nothing. He was hard put to understand what man would want her anyway. She had the morals of a mink and the flightiness of a feather; a coal field queen with lots of mileage on her.

Terry bent and extended his hand to help his fellow climbers gain the last obstacle.

"Wait. Quiet! I thought I heard something," Terry said.

This time, the stillness was broken by a whispering and chilly wind. Here and there along the ridge, the air movement rattled leafless tree limbs together. It was a dull, dead sound like sticks against a muffled drum. Still on the level below Terry, Dowless called out, "What did you think you heard?"

"I could swear to God I heard a baby's cry when I first got up here."

"Can you see the outline of the eagle's nest?" Stanford asked.

After a pause, Terry said, "No. Didn't the chopper pilot say it was in a tree beside a tall column of rock?"

"Yeah," Dowless said. "When we all get on top, let's get our eyes adjusted to the light and spread out, then we can find that juttin' pedestal. No use in lookin' in trees until we find that rock spire."

Dowless was just gaining the peak when Terry and another hiker called out almost simultaneously: "There it is again. I heard it. If that's not a baby's cry, then it's got to be a bobcat or a skunk, one," Terry added.

That was stretching the point a mile, Dowless thought. While it was true that a bobcat and a skunk could imitate a woman's cry, the sound of an infant's wailing was distinctive and unique.

"You're just gettin' the jitters," someone out of the dark said.

"Maybe it's time we all got the jitters," Terry countered, "because if there are bobcats around, they may be headed for that eagle's nest, too, And I don't imagine they'll be too particular about whether they eat baby eagles or regular. . ."

Although Terry had stopped his words short, the point was all too clear. Above and beyond that new worry, there was a rising wind that was getting colder by the minute.

To the utter amazement of all, the night seemed to be getting brighter rather than darker. Their eyes had adjusted well, of course, but aside from that, a degree of light from the moon struck the polished surface of the rocks and reflected a kind of blue-white light. The face of every man, Dowless noticed, took on a kind of pewter hue.

Sheriff Stanford was the first man to spot the pinnacle over which the chopper had hovered. Nevertheless, Stanford instructed everyone to hold back while he and Groves advanced. Dowless didn't have to ask why. Whoever had pumped those slugs into the helicopter might still be around. If the hostile force was a clan of moonshiners, the chances were good they were now long gone. They would have sense enough to reason that although they had downed the chopper, by daylight there would be an army coming after them.

Stanford and Groves advanced cautiously farther along the crest. Both men had prudently not used their flashlights. Dowless could see the two law officers stop in their tracks, and in a moment more, he saw a quick reflection of moonlight from the service revolvers both men had drawn. Evidently, they had heard something. Dowless could hear the breath of every man around him. They had all been huffing and puffing from the climb, but now all of their breath was halting and sporadic. They waited.

Dowless was surprised that the onrush of sudden fear had seemed to sharpen his eyesight. He saw both law officers holster their weapons. Stanford focused his flashlight beam up a shaft of rock, trailed it off to his right, and there it was: a huge eagle's nest of sticks and leaves, and it looked as big around as a zinc washtub. Groves sighted in his flashlight, too, and Dowless and the others started forward. Dowless had not taken ten steps before a burst of gunfire split the night. Either Stanford's or Groves' flashlight had hit the rocks or been shattered by rifle fire. The remaining light went black. Even so, a second short burst of rifle fire resounded and brought down a shower of severed branches. There was no dirt to hit, but Dowless and every man around him went belly down against the rocks.

"Stanford? Groves? You guys okay?" Dowless kept his voice as low as he could.

"Yeah, we're both all right," Stanford responded in a shaky voice little above a whisper. "Can you snake across the rocks with that beer belly of yours? We've got a problem. We better talk it over."

When Dowless edged up to the two law officers, he had sanded off the buttons of his jacket and a sliver of rock had cut through his shirt down along his belly. He couldn't see the wound, but his fingertips felt warm residue. Stanford let Dowless breathe to ease himself for a moment, and then he said, "We've got a bigger problem than you think. I don't know how much you know about weaponry, but we're not being shot at by a .22 or your ordinary hardware store deer rifle. That's heavy artillery down in those trees."

"What do you mean?" Dowless asked.

"Automatic, or semi-automatic, weaponry," Stanford said.

"Military stuff, most likely," Groves added.

As though the enemy was annoyed by the long silence, three quick bursts of fire broke the stillness. The bright orange flame from the muzzle of the weapon cast dancing silhouettes against the rocks.

Terry Binns and two of the other hikers snaked along the ledge to where Dowless and the two lawmen were taking cover.

"Whoever he is, he means business," Terry said.

"That brings up an important point," Stanford said. "Two service revolvers are no match for his artillery, but maybe we better let him—or them—know we've got something to fight back with."

"Them? You really think there's a whole gang of them in there?" Dowless asked.

"How the hell would I know?" Stanford grunted. "We don't know what we've got. Didn't Captain Slater infer on the radio that when the chopper took on fire that it was from multiple weapons?"

"I don't remember," Dowless confessed. "Everything happened so quickly, and then his voice was gone, and I can't remember his exact words."

"Aren't we all forgettin' our original mission?" Groves asked. "It's got to be gettin' cold up in that eagle's nest, and what if that mama bird is settin' up there usin' that razor beak and claws?"

"Oh, God," Dowless groaned.

"Where are those baby cries you thought you heard earlier?" Stanford whispered to Terry. "Does it occur to anybody else except me that if that baby was up there and alive that gun fire would have brought its lungs to life?"

The observation was all too true. Everyone was wordless, and for a moment their combined breaths sounded like great bellows.

"I think it's time to announce ourselves," Stanford said. "Keep your heads down." Stanford drew his service revolver and three quick shots rang out. The sound of the revolver sounded ten times louder than the earlier rifle fire, but perhaps it was their proximity to the revolver, Dowless reasoned. Nevertheless, no sooner had the blasts died away than an infant's wailing pierced the darkness. The little lungs were strong, and from the tenor of the voice, the baby sounded as mad as mischief. Dowless did a double take. The cries were coming from beyond the ledge at the base of some trees—not up over their heads in the eagle's nest. Outlined in the moonlight, Dowless could see the heads of the other men going first to the eagle's nest and then back to the sound of the child's cry.

"What in the devil is going on here?" Stanford grunted. "Whoever they are, they've got the child. . ."

That was obvious to everyone. Who, how, and why was another matter. They didn't have time to debate it. Somebody held his finger on the trigger and dropped tree limbs with a spew of bullets across a wide parameter.

"This is Sheriff Otto Stanford. Lay down your weaponry and come out into the moonlight. We didn't come after you! We came after the baby."

There was no response, and Groves whispered, "We didn't have to announce ourselves. He could see our shiny faces, and chances are good, he was waitin'."

"This is Sheriff Otto Stanford. I don't know what your game is, and right now I don't care. Lay the baby out in the moonlight where we can see it and go on about your business. You won't be harmed. If you're running illegal liquor or distributing dope from a cave, this time it don't matter. We just want the kid."

Again, the silence hung.

"Keep your heads down," Stanford ordered. "Groves, turn your flashlight beam on and off real quick in the direction of that sound."

Groves did as ordered, but there was not time to see anything. A couple of bursts of hot lead came closer than before, and Groves swore that he could feel the heat from the projectiles.

"He may be pinning us down," Stanford said, "but it's for certain he's not trying to kill us. He could have gotten us all while we were outlined against the sky like a bunch of ducks in a shooting gallery."

In ones and twos, the men further back edged closer, seeking more knowledge of just what was going on.

"We'll tell you when we know," Dowless said. "There's somethin' funny goin' on back in those trees. If we're up against druggies or shiners, it doesn't make sense that they would down a chopper that hadn't seen them anyway, and call a whole army in on themselves."

"We're beginning to think alike," Stanford said.

"You sayin' we got some kind of nut on our hands?" Groves asked.

Before anyone could answer, the child's wailing stopped too suddenly. The little boy's captor had undoubtedly clapped a hand across his mouth to silence him. In another minute, however, the child was squawling again with even greater volume. It had been a long time since Dowless had been around a newborn, but if he was any judge, that baby was as mad as a wet hen. Still, the crying said something: the child's captor was at least humane enough not to suffocate it. Dowless called out, "What do you want with a hungry, wounded little boy, anyway? His mama and daddy are half dead with worry, and if you don't have sense enough to know it, the kid's goin' to get a bad case of frostbite."

There was a momentary rustle in the dry leaves well below them, but no discernible form stepped out from among the trees.

"My child is warm," a male voice announced. "My

hands are marked with its blood, but I've patched his wounds. Don't you think I've got sense enough to take care of my own?"

As though to emphasize the point, the speaker sent a barrage of bullets into the rocks and the whining ricochettes echoed from pinnacle to pinnacle.

"Who are you?" Stanford demanded. "Identify yourself!"

"Who am I?" the voice mocked. "You know who I am. Otherwise, why've you come back for me?"

Dowless caught at once the strangeness of the voice and the slow articulation of each word that the speaker uttered. The voice was like a dramatic reading.

"What do you mean 'my own'?" Stanford demanded. "The little boy, Joshua, you have, is the only son of a local miner and his wife. The child was stolen by an eagle and dropped in the nest where you found him."

"No, my friends," the voice called back with deliberate calmness, "the baby has been delivered to me by a merciful angel. The child is the sign of my redemption."

"Redemption from what?" Dowless asked. "Bring the child to us, then we'll talk."

"No. You don't understand. The child is mine, and I'll look after him and love him. I'll make it up to him, and everything will be all right," the voice trailed off.

Dowless and Stanford started to confer, but in that same moment they heard low weeping coming out of the darkness. The weeping brought the child's voice to life again, and Dowless wondered how the infant could possibly wail any more. It had now been over seven hours since the eagle had snatched him away, and longer than that since he'd feasted on his mother's milk. Stanford interrupted Dowless' thoughts.

"How do you read it—Dowless? Groves? You think we got some kind of nut treed?"

"Sounds like it," Groves said.

"Somethin' unusual in the air. That's for sure," Dowless said. "We're in your county, Stanford. You know about any hermits living up here? Maybe we've uncovered a druggie's den. That description fit anybody from your county that you can think of?"

"Hell, yes," Stanford said. "About twenty percent of the population, but nothing fits for here that I can think of."

"Well, whatever the situation is, we sure can't shoot at him," Groves said. "The way he's talkin', he may have the baby in one arm and shootin' with the other."

Stanford thought for a minute and then he said, "Even when dawn comes, and if we can separate him from the baby, we're no match for him with the kind of fire power he's got. We'd better radio out for more of my deputies, and Groves, you're going to need more of your people up here. We'd better get more state police in on this, and maybe they can come in from the direction of Interstate 75. If they can scale that side of the mountain, then we'll have this looney bird surrounded."

Dowless and Groves agreed with the move, and Dowless further realized that the second wave of search and rescue volunteers would be coming up the mountain without any kind of beacon guidance.

While Stanford tried to establish radio contact with his deputy down at roadside, Dowless and Terry slid off the rock, walked down the mountainside a way to be out of range of any flying bullets, and wedged their activated flashlights in tree limbs. In this wilderness, Dowless thought, a lighted match would serve as guidance.

When Dowless and Terry crawled back up the rock face, Stanford was having no luck. Apparently, the deputy was not near enough to his vehicle to hear the call. Undoubtedly, the deputy had gone with the stretcher bearers to the site of the downed chopper. Thank God, there had been no explosion, but that didn't mean that it still couldn't come with a thunderous roar. Within a fleeting moment, Dowless wondered if ambulance drivers—if indeed they had arrived on the scene—would find a single living man to rush to the hospital.

Stanford gave up his attempted transmissions. Dowless knew that neither his radio nor Deputy Groves', in

73

the shielded location in which they now found themselves, would have the range to reach back to Corbin. Mention of the fact prompted Stanford to try something different.

"You guys all stay here and just sit tight," Stanford ordered. "Don't make any new waves and I'll try to snake back out along the north side of the mountain. I'm closer to home than you guys from Corbin, and if I can get out from under this shelf and out to a high peak, I can reach my office dispatcher. He can get things going and call Corbin as well."

Above all else, Dowless had looked forward to coming off the mountain with the child in his arms. Second to that was being able to get advance word to Maria and Joe Fremont that their child was alive and not mortally wounded. He suggested to Stanford that if he could reach his dispatcher that word be relayed to the Fremonts at once.

Stanford hesitated unduly long, then said, "Why hand them two tragedies in one day? They're already reconciled to the fact that their son may be dead. We all know that he's alive now, but the longer that nut who has him thinks about the hopelessness of his situation, the more desperate he's going to get."

"What do you mean?" Dowless asked.

"Try this on for size: that junkie—or whatever he is—down in the woods yonder, is going to figure out that when daylight comes, he's had it. He's not about to leave the baby and run. He says the boy is 'his.' Even if the nut wasn't having hallucinations, he would certainly use the child as an insurance policy. It's going to be tough going carrying a baby and whatever weapons he's got with him. Suppose he stuffs that child in his jacket and ties him in some way. Then just suppose somebody gets trigger happy and takes a shot at him not knowing that the child is lying against his chest? I think you get the picture. We don't have any assurance at all that that baby will ever leave these mountains alive."

Dowless knew that everything Stanford said was true.

He himself had simply not been able to come to terms with this new and dangerous dilemma. He wanted only to see Joshua Fremont back in the arms of his mother and father. And if Dowless knew Joe Fremont as he thought he did, the bull-strong miner was on his way to make his own contribution in the rescue of his son.

Dowless watched Stanford move off as quickly as conditions allowed. The lawman inched his long body with surprising agility along the ledge, but when his hand or foot dislodged a loose stone, the noise was amplified in the still night. The sound and its direction of origin invited a continuous burst of fire that seemed minutes long in duration.

"You're not going to get me!" the voice that was measured before now sounded panicky.

In the pause, Stanford had crawled from view, and no one uttered a sound.

"You're not taking me back!" the desperate voice was going higher still. "Hell, no! I won't go!"

The outburst was repeated like a child chanting phrases of mockery, and then the voice broke and resolved itself with low sobs. For a moment, Dowless questioned his own sanity. He could see on the moonlit faces of the men about him that they, too, were disquieted and confused.

The voice among the trees began alternating between sobs and unintelligible rantings. Sometimes Dowless could understand a few words, but the obvious agony and confusion of the speaker distorted meanings and spat out incomplete phrases. Dowless could tell by the utterances that the speaker paced back and forth as though his spine was electrified and his feet on fire.

The infant's voice had not been heard now for fully five minutes. Dowless wondered if it had somehow smothered itself, or if its captor had been inattentive enough to invite suffocation. Maybe the baby was just plain exhausted, and if so, it would be a blessing in disguise. What a trooper Joshua Fremont had been, Dowless thought, but he quickly changed 'had been' to 'is.'

The muttering in the distance slowed and became well articulated again.

"You'll never get me back to Nam. You stole my mind and you ripped out my heart and my balls, too. You made me kill people I didn't want to kill, and they visit me sometimes and ask me why I did it. Make them go away!"

Dowless began to feel something he had not felt before. Beyond what he had heard and deciphered, it was a kind of instinctive awareness. Could there be one small shred of kindness in this wild man who screamed out at them? Dowless gambled in spite of Stanford's instruction to the contrary.

"None of us have anything to do with the military," Dowless called out clearly. "We're tellin' you the truth. We just climbed up here to rescue the baby, that's all. We want to take Joshua back to his mother. Have you harmed the infant? Why haven't we heard it cryin'?"

"Because he's sleeping, that's why," the voice called back angrily. "He's at peace. Why can't you be? Just go away and leave me and my child alone."

"But he isn't your child," Dowless called back calmly.

"It is! It is! I've told you that before. Why don't you listen? The little boy is the sign of my redemption, you ought to know that. Now get it straight this time!"

The words were followed by the slow firing of a weapon unlike the ones used before. The sounds of the shots spaced apart as they were, were exceedingly loud.

Deputy Groves eased over to Dowless' side and said, "I'd know that sound anywhere. That's a 45 automatic. I don't know who that guy is, but he's got one hell of an arsenal down there. If we're smart, we won't do anything until dawn, and until we have plenty of reinforcements."

The infant's protests echoed through the trees, but this time Dowless could discern a choking weariness in the child's cries. As the little boy tried to draw breath at intervals, a rattling sound emerged from his throat.

When Stanford returned reporting success, Dowless made a suggestion: they must do nothing to draw more gun fire. Sleep for the infant was now vital. Perhaps rest would overcome hunger and fatigue and insure survival throughout the night.

As though assistance were already arriving, Dowless heard a strange fluttering sound. The noise was not at ground level. When he looked up, the silhouette of a great bird coming to rest on the rim of her nest could be seen. Dowless still doubted that eagles travelled at night, and if he was right, he marvelled still more at the depth of a mother's love. The flutter of wings drew no gun fire, but maybe the child's captor had seen the same scene and was drawing a sympathetic parallel.

As warming as that thought was to Dowless, he was quickly jerked back into the real world. The faint whine of sirens could be heard in the distance. Had Captain Paul Slater and his crew survived? Dowless doubted it unless the chopper had come down on a very soft cushion of trees. He hoped so. In his experience, first victims in a tragedy were only a prelude of more to come.

CHAPTER VIII

Deputy Austin Wheelwright had gotten off easy. It had been simple enough to sit in the warm squad car at the intersection and act as traffic director and radio relay man, but when that chopper came tumbling out of the sky, the pace of things changed considerably. At times, he had been able to observe the hovering aircraft in the distance, and its spot and warning lights looking so eerie against the night sky had made it look like a banana-shaped spacecraft getting ready to squat on top of the world.

He hadn't been able to tell exactly when the pilot had begun to lose control, or whether some malfunction had caused the machine to start its earthward plunge. Like a thrown flat stone skipping across calm water, the chopper slid from pine grove to pine grove, taking the tops of trees as it went. Not until the disabled craft had travelled in this manner for what he estimated to be a quarter of a mile, then slammed into a crescent-shaped grove of mature hemlock trees, did it finally settle to earth. For a moment he had thought his eyes were playing tricks on him.

Wheelwright jumped back into the cruiser, backed out onto the county road, and headed in the direction of the crash. As best he could tell, the chopper had come down some four hundred to six hundred yards northeast of his position. He flipped on his flashers and en route radioed in for ambulances and extra paramedics. Otto Stanford and the advance rescue party on the mountain had seen the chopper fall, of course, and he wondered what new obstacles the loss of the chopper would pose for the searchers. He tried making radio contact with Stanford but got no reply. He found himself wondering if some kind of new emergency on the mountain prevailed and thus had kept radio traffic to a minimum. Some flicker of instinct told him that something unusual was going on. At 32, he had a great deal to learn about law enforcement, but sometimes he could smell trouble. Now, there was little purpose in the instinctive feeling for the volunteers were miles removed, while he was here in the flat lands with a king-sized emergency on his hands.

At several places along the road, he stopped and got out to orient himself. At any point along the stretch, the downed chopper, judging by the only warning light that was now visible among the trees, was still 200-300 yards away. Wheelwright left his flashers on to guide the ambulance crews and anybody else who happened to be speeding along the road. He grabbed his flashlight, started to exit the vehicle, then doubled back for a small fire extinguisher.

For a time, he trotted across the terrain, but the farther he travelled, the more dense the underbrush became. He circumvented a line of thorn trees, but not before he had felt their sharp stinging against his outer thigh. The stabbing sensation felt like it had penetrated to the bone. For once he'd like to have been well insulated, but his physique was lean.

At just over the halfway point to the crash site, his flashlight beam picked up a small stream no wider than his squad car. Once across it, he saw the outline of the disabled craft.

Closer up, the warning lights on the chopper started to fade off and on as though a short circuit was occurring in the wiring. Unbelievably, a young man in sergeant's stripes stood outside the chopper, but judging by his halting steps, he was either injured or dazed. The blinking lights of the chopper created the eerie effect of flashing neon, and the first red, then green, lips of the sergeant tried to form a coherent sentence but faltered, and he pointed toward the exit door. Wheelwright played his light beam over the craft, and it was not as completely demolished as he might have supposed. The rotor was gone, the nose compacted, and the underbelly had numerous gashes across it, but it had not been squashed from top to bottom.

The exit door stood ajar, and he crawled up and through the opening. He heard no moans in the dark cabin, but he did get a whiff of burning or melting rubber. Even so, he saw no flames and breathed a sigh of relief. Wedged between the pilot's seat and the control panel was a man with captain's bars, either dead or unconscious. Wheelwright put his cheek to the man's nostrils and discovered that he was still breathing. On the opposite side of the forward cabin, a man with lieutenant's bars lay in a contorted position. It was quickly evident that just below his knees both legs were broken. A faint moan escaped his lips, and a trickle of blood oozed from his mouth. Rearward, at the hoist control station, a corporal lay on the floor, alive but out cold.

Wheelwright loosened the shirt collars of the men and pondered what was best to do. He felt helpless until the ambulance crews arrived, and he knew that to move the wounded men in any way might hurt rather than help them. He did, however, brace his back against the instrument panel and with one foot against the pilot's seat, spring it backward to lessen the pressure against the unconscious man's chest. He then looked around for some type of covering in order to keep the wounded men as warm as possible. During that duty, he again caught a whiff of smoldering rubber, insulation, or some other material. He debated the wisdom of first giving every nook and cranny a blast from his fire extinguisher.

He jumped down to the ground and found the sergeant standing again.

"Are you sure you're all right?" Wheelwright asked.

"After I get over the shakes, I will be," the sergeant said.

"All of your buddies in there are hurt pretty bad. I don't know whether they'll make it or not, but a couple of ambulances are on the way."

"They've got to make it," the sergeant said more steadily, "we're all friends—we work together all the time."

"What happened? How did you lose control?"

"Some maniac up on top of the mountain tried to shoot us down. Guess you could say he did."

Wheelwright was so startled that he wondered if the dazed sergeant could be imagining things. Nobody in the rescue group would have shot at anything, and besides, no one except Otto Stanford and the other deputy likely had weapons.

"Are you sure you were shot at?" Wheelwright pressed.

"Hell, yes, I'm sure. If you don't believe me, shine your light back across the fuselage and look closely."

Wheelwright did so, and he could see the pock marks of expended bullets here and there. Looked at casually, the holes could be mistaken for rivets.

"Whoever that sniper was, he damaged our rotor as well," the sergeant added.

Wheelwright backed off. His flashlight beam caught the expression of anger that passed over the Guardsman's face.

"From what I see, we're talking about automatic weapons fire," Wheelwright said.

"No doubt about it. No country squirrel hunter with a gun blazing in each hand could put that number of shell holes into a craft unless he had a military type weapon."

"It doesn't make any sense. There's nobody up there that would. . ."

". . .obviously, there is. You sure there're no fugitives from justice around here? Anybody you know of on the run that might think the law is looking for him?"

"No. Nobody in particular. Of course, somebody is always on the run. Still doesn't make sense, though."

"I'm just a weekend soldier. This kind of thing isn't supposed to happen. I'm a coach, not some kind of mercenary with an itchy trigger finger. It's a real challenge to swing down in that basket and pluck somebody off a burning building or out of raging water, but shooting or getting shot at doesn't appeal to me a damn bit."

Wheelwright again caught a whiff of something smoldering. He couldn't tell where it was coming from for certain, and there was not the slightest flicker of flame anywhere.

"I think for safety's sake, we'd better try and get your three buddies out of there and hose the whole place down with fire extinguishers. I brought one and I suppose you have plenty inside?" Wheelwright said.

The sergeant had caught the smell, and he too was sniffing the night air. He was still shaking either from the shock or from the deepening chill of the night breeze.

"Don't guess we have any choice. What's left of Bertha could go up in flames at any minute."

"Is that what you call her?" Wheelwright chuckled.

"Yeah. Big Bertha's been on many a mission."

Both of them crawled through the doorway, and the sergeant flipped on a dome light. After a minute, the light flickered off and on, then went out completely. Wheelwright used his flashlight again, and nothing had changed. The captain was still breathing, but barely. The lieutenant's groans were louder which was a good sign. The corporal was still out. With the sergeant's help, Wheelwright slowly, carefully straightened the lieutenant's body out along the floor so he could breathe more easily.

"There are more blankets back in the tail section," the sergeant said. "We carry lots of them in rescue work. We'll have to fashion a blanket stretcher, but it sure isn't going to be easy getting these guys down to the ground."

With the utmost ease, they had worked the lieutenant onto the blanket and slid him along the floor toward the exit door. Somehow, the wounded man's legs would need to be splinted before they lifted him to the ground. Wheelwright hopped to earth and began a search among the split trees and splintered limbs surrounding the aircraft. Numerous slats of varying widths and lengths were quickly found. When he returned, the sergeant had a roll of tape ready.

"Can you crawl around in the dark and find things?" Wheelwright chuckled.

"First rule of the game in the rescue business. Know where everything is, even if you have to find it in the dark."

They started the task of splinting the two injured legs, but with makeshift light, and clumsy, inexperienced hands, the progress was slow. In the pause, the distant sound of a siren broke the silence. Wheelwright jumped down to the ground immediately.

"Let's wait and let the professionals do it. Sit tight. I'm goin' to climb a tree and guide them in with my flashlight beam. They'll be as frustrated as hell that they can't get the vehicles close up. . ."

En route from the highway, the first paramedics were slowed only momentarily when one of them fell in the branch that Wheelwright had crossed over. They had good portable lighting of their own, but from his perch halfway up a leafless oak tree, Wheelwright kept jiggling his own flashlight to keep them on course. As the paramedics trudged onward, the wailing siren of a second ambulance could be heard in the distance.

As quickly as the pros had the wounded men out of the chopper attending them on the ground, Wheelwright and the sergeant went to work with the fire extinguishers. They soon had the interior coated as though it had undergone a dusting of snow, but Wheelwright wondered if all of their effort would do the job. Next, they walked around the craft and observed minute puffs of smoke drifting out through the slits in the chopper's underbelly. They exhausted the contents of their last fire extinguisher into the suspect area, but the smoldering smell did not dissipate. A cocky paramedic from the Corbin crew—whom Wheelwright had never met—began injecting his opinions with regard to fire prevention.

"Your efforts may dampen things down a little bit, but you've got a ticking time bomb, there. Why don't you let me dispatch a couple of fire trucks out here so they can be on standby?"

The sergeant agreed. "There must be 2,000 miles of wire in that thing. It'll only take two of them arcing in the right place to start a fire, and there'll be no stopping its spread."

"You're forgetting something," Wheelwright reminded. "How you goin' to get the trucks over here?"

"Those fire engines ought to have plenty of axle clearance as big as their wheels are. They could at least get across the rough terrain as far as the branch. They're going to need more water than they can carry anyway, so why can't they suck it out of the branch and arch it over among the trees?" the paramedic said.

It was precautionary advice too good to ignore and Wheelwright approved it. It meant, of course, that he would have to stay on station where he was until the fire trucks arrived. It quickly occurred to him also that it had been too long since he'd made radio contact with Otto Stanford, his boss.

The sergeant was willing to stay and assist in any way he could, but the paramedics insisted that he come with them for a thorough checkup at the clinic in Corbin. The paramedics had found bruises and cuts on the sergeant's body that he'd been unaware of. When the three seriously wounded men were ready for stretcher bearing, Wheelwright ventured one last question: "What are their chances?"

"All of them are hanging on by the skin of their teeth. You can't ever tell. It depends on how much gut-deep fight they've got left in themselves. Radio on in later, and we'll give you an update."

Wheelwright followed along to lend his assistance as they all departed the scene. A couple of state police cruisers were just arriving.

As the ambulances sped off, Wheelwright returned to his cruiser and reached for the mike. Somebody responded to the call, but interference obliterated clarity. Wheelwright asked the respondent to move to a higher and less obstructed point to clear up the static.

Otto Stanford's voice soon came in clearly. "What's the story on the men in the chopper?"

"One of them is in good shape. The other three are in a bad way. The medics say they may not make it."

"Some of us may not make it either. We've got a lunatic armed to the teeth up here. Apparently, he's got an arsenal of military type weapons. As you probably know by now, it was him that brought the chopper down."

"Yeah. The NG sergeant—the one who was not hurt badly—told me about it. I could see for myself enough bullet holes to down a fighter plane. Have you found out the gunman's name?"

"The bastard hasn't said much of anything that makes sense," Stanford said. "Seems like he wants to back up every other statement he makes with a burst of gunfire. I don't know whether he's a druggie or just plain crazy, or both."

"What about the baby? Is the gunman between you and the nest, or have you been able to send someone on an end run?"

"You're not going to believe this, but the gunman's got the baby. Claims it's his. Some kind of heaven-sent gift or something. He's not making any sense at all."

Wheelwright gulped. No, he couldn't believe it, but his boss had just told him so.

"Shouldn't I go ahead and touch base with the dispatcher? Let him telephone the parents? It'd give them some relief just to know that the kid is alive."

"I decided against that but I'm getting a lot of arm twisting up here," Stanford said. "I was holding back because I'm not so sure we're going to get the infant out of here alive. Looks like I'm getting overruled, though. Everybody up here thinks we ought to dish out the hope as long as any hope exists."

"Then you want to go ahead and have the Fremonts notified?"

"We may live to regret it, but yeah, go ahead and get them word. By the way, we sent half of our force down the mountain to help you untangle that chopper and get the guardsmen out. Guess it was a fool's mission, and they haven't had time to get down there anyway, but we didn't know what your situation would be."

"Since the chopper didn't burn and they had no light to guide them, the odds are good that they're lost somewhere between here and there."

"Well, if and when they do get down there, just tell them to rest for a while. There's nothing they can do up here right now, and I can't ask them to climb the mountain twice in one night."

"As you say. . ."

"Speaking of flames, you sure that chopper isn't still going to blow? That's all we'd need: to have the whole mountain turned into a torch."

"I can't tell you whether it will go up or not, but the lights on the thing flickered for a long time, then went out. I could smell burning rubber or insulation or something, but we used every fire extinguisher we had to hose it down. As an added precaution, a couple of fire trucks are going to come on out and remain on standby."

"Good thinking," Stanford said. "By the way, have any other groups of volunteers started up the mountain?"

"About an hour before I had to pull off station a small group came in late but I didn't know any of them. I don't know who or how many might have gone by after I headed for the crash scene."

"Well, I guess it doesn't matter, but there's nothing any of them can help with now, and too many just might make matters worse."

"What do you mean?" Wheelwright asked.

"It's a volatile situation up here. Big numbers might just set this lunatic into a frenzy. The guy keeps babbling about the war in Viet Nam. I think he's too much off his rocker to know that the war has been long over."

"Shell shocked vet, maybe? All the bad dreams coming back?"

"Could be. I hear tell that it's happening more and more."

"Anything else before I sign off?" Wheelwright asked.

"Go ahead and touch base again with the KSP. Make sure they're on the move and remind them that at dawn, I'll be expecting a force coming up the Interstate 75 side of the mountain. Give them an update and tell them to proceed with caution. I'll keep in contact by radio from here when they come into range."

"I'm glad it's not me tryin' to scale up that side of the mountain. A man would have to be about half mountain goat. . ."

"Well, if they need a lesson in toughness, I'll give them one. There's a little fellow up here who's given us all a good lesson. We haven't heard him wailing for a while now, but the last time he did sing out, he was mad as a charging bull. Guess he wonders, too, why nobody will change his dirty diapers."

"Hang in there," Wheelwright said.

"We're a hungry and tired bunch, but it won't be long before dawn. Maybe a temporary cease fire is good for all of us. Over and out."

* * *

Joe Fremont and the volunteers who had accompanied him were well up the mountainside when they heard the sirens and got an occasional glimpse at the flashing red lights along the highway in the far distance. They all took a breather for a moment and pondered. Joe continued to be puzzled by the scene, but the collective opinion seemed to be that the commotion had nothing to do with the search activities along the mountaintop. The supposition seemed reasonable, and yet Joe felt a moment of disquiet. No one among them had a radio, and for the moment, they were literally in the dark. Although he could see small shafts of light coming from trees near the mountain crest, the absence of a hovering helicopter suddenly hit him. He had been given to understand that a chopper was keeping watch over the eagle's nest. The light he could see was obviously suspended lanterns placed there to guide oncoming rescue workers, but did the absent aircraft imply that his child had already been rescued and the National Guard crewsmen sent home? God only knew how he wanted to believe that, but the greater likelihood was that little Joshua had not survived the ordeal.

A whimper escaped his throat, and he moved off a way from the others to mourn in private. Real men didn't cry. He hated the sounds coming from himself, and he wanted to take his own big strong hands and constrict his throat to make it stop.

By sheer will, he turned his mourning into physical strength and lengthened his strides to catch up with the others.

When they reached a hump on the hill that looked in silhouette like a vast wart, they could see lights moving through the trees just a few hundred yards above them. Joe urged his fellow hikers to greater speed in hopes of catching up with the earlier group. Maybe someone had a radio and had heard what was going on.

The catching up was easier to imagine then to accomplish. The higher group was moving determinedly upward.

"Wait! Does anybody have a radio?" Joe called out to the limit of his lungs.

"Yeah," a vaguely familiar voice called back in equal volume.

"Hold up then," Joe called back.

Joe half ran, half stumbled to close the distance. Close up, he darted his flashlight beam left to right and saw the somber faces of many of his friends and coworkers. Spider Cornett took a step toward him. Joe had worked with the gangly miner for almost five years, and the two of them had been friends for the same length of time. They played ball together, and shared many a beer and bull session.

Joe's flashlight beam picked up the outline of the radio at Spider's belt, and he asked, "Have you heard anything? Have they reached the eagle's nest yet? What about the chopper. . ."

"We just picked up a transmission between the mountaintop and a squad car down the highway. Joshua is alive but he's bein' held captive by somebody off his nut.

The guy is well armed and he shot the chopper down."

Spider elaborated on the other details he'd caught during the transmission.

"But has anybody gotten word to Maria?" Joe interrupted after a moment.

"Yeah," Spider said, "the deputy's gettin' word to her right now."

For a moment the good news seemed to paralyze Joe, but just as quickly a flood of joy sent him leaping into the air with a cowboy yell that ran up and down the face of the mountain. He grabbed Spider in a crushing embrace, then lifted him from the ground.

"Joshua's alive! My boy's alive! Thank God I'll hold him again and I can tell you this right now: he'll never want for anything as long as he lives."

"I don't mean to dampen your spirits none," a voice came out of the darkness, "but gettin' your baby back from a lunatic may be harder than snatchin' him out of an eagle's nest."

"I don't know who this lunatic is, or how he happened to be up in the mountains, but I can tell you this," Joe said, "if he harms one hair of Joshua's head, I'll break every bone in his body."

"And I'll help you," Spider said.

Everybody moved off, and Joe tried to keep up and stay at Spider's side. In less than fifty yards, Joe was pleading to slow down. Spider shortened his stride, and Joe could tell that his friend was deep in thought.

Finally, Spider said, "I still can't shake it off. I didn't mean to shoo those damn birds over on you. . ." Spider's voice began to break. Nevertheless, he let out a string of oaths as though to relieve the pent-up anger and self shame he felt. Ordinarily, Spider didn't cuss a great deal except when things frustrated him. The choice of curse words somehow seemed out of keeping with the peace and quiet that now engulfed them.

"I should have shot those goddamn birds," Spider muttered anew.

"Guess we've got a lot to be thankful for after all. The

good news. . .the good smell of the mountain, here. . .it's all kind of a holy moment—you know? Gets a man to thinkin'."

"Didn't mean to sound so irreverent. Hard for me to be anything but my natural self, though. You and me've been through a lot together, and I'm the one that brought trouble down on you."

Joe gave Spider a slap across the back and said, "Put that out of your mind. Everything's going to work out all right, you'll see. . ."

* * *

On top of the mountain, it was getting chillier by the hour. Dowless, Stanford, and Groves huddled together, and their coworkers sat close by. Everybody was taking a moment now and then to peep over the top of the rocky breastworks to see if any movement was taking place along the tree line below. No one had heard anything more than an occasional rustle of leaves. Maybe, even, the baby's captor had the good sense to fashion a warm leaf bed, Dowless hoped. He voiced the comforting thought to Stanford, but the sheriff was already ahead of him.

"Maybe that's what the sounds of those rustling leaves mean, but on the other hand, it may be a subterfuge. I'm trying to think like *he* might be thinking. Time's running out for him, and he probably knows that."

"I'm not sure he's thinkin'—or can think—with any kind of normal judgment," Dowless said.

"Somehow or other, the criminal part of the mind always manages to stay healthy," Groves opined.

"I just hope he'll let the baby sleep and regain some strength before dawn," Dowless said.

"I wouldn't if I was him," Stanford said. "I'd be thinking about getting out of here before dawn broke. He knows how to get around in the dark a whole lot better than we do. Somewhere not too far away is his cave, or private bush arbor; he's at home up here. We're the intruders."

"I'd like to have a little bit of his grub and hot coffee right now," Groves said.

"Amen," a murmur went down the line.

"That's part of my point," Stanford said. "He's got to be getting hungry, too. And I don't care if he has made himself a leaf bed. If he's got his jacket wrapped around that baby like he claims, he's feelin' the frost on his hide like we are. He'll make a run for it, I tell you, and if he's smart, he'll do it before dawn."

Dowless knew the sheriff was probably right, but he couldn't bear to think of anything happening that would disturb Joshua's sleep.

"We've got another problem to think of, too, before dawn gets here," Groves reminded. "We've got this lunatic flanked on the east, and by dawn the KSP should have the west covered, but we're going to have to send out flankers to the south and north of us."

"That hadn't slipped my mind," Stanford said a little stiffly, "but I'm not about to send unarmed civilians out as flankers. I'm counting on those extra deputies we radioed for, getting up here before dawn. I don't expect them to be very happy about rolling out of bed to do a double shift, but they'll be here."

"It'll sure as hell be slow going," Groves said. "It was tough gettin' my beer belly up that mountain by itself, much less an extra shotgun and a sniper's rifle like those boys will be carrying."

"You suppose there's any chance of callin' in another chopper?" Dowless asked. "Sure would be nice to have some help from above—to help in trackin' the fugitive if nothing else."

"I don't imagine the National Guard's going to be very happy about losing one chopper—and some of the men in it, maybe—so it won't prove a thing to get a second one shot down. Of course, maybe when daylight comes, we could have one on standby that could stay at a safe range and give us some assistance. Let me get on my radio and see if we can set that up."

Stanford's voice seemed amplified in the night, but the

confirming voice jumping out of the squawking receiver seemed magnified one hundred times. No sooner had Stanford pocketed his radio than rustling leaves in the distance could be heard. Footsteps were slow but distinct. Cat-like, the walker slowly approached the breastworks of his enemy without apparent fear or hesitation.

"I don't think he likes the sound of my radio," Stanford whispered. "He's going to let loose with a blast, I can feel it. When I give the signal, throw your light beams on him. I want a look at that dude, and maybe for a split second we can blind him as well."

"Why can't we pick him off if he doesn't have the baby in his arms?" Groves asked.

"You that good a shot with a .38 at this distance?" Stanford challenged.

"No, but we might get lucky."

"And we might all get our heads chopped off with a spew of bullets from that M-16 or whatever he's got," Stanford said.

"I don't think we ought to shoot him even if we have the chance," Dowless said.

"Why the hell not?" Groves replied.

"I don't know. There's just somethin' about him . . . maybe I'm imaginin' things'" Dowless said. "What if he's a war vet . . . just a little sick, maybe . . ."

"He's still a kidnapper," Stanford said. "It's the same whether he steals a kid from a house or an eagle's nest."

"I can't put my finger on it, but there's somethin' different here," Dowless said.

"I still think we ought to disable him if we get the openin'," Groves insisted. "Joe Fremont would expect us to gun the guy down if that's what it took to free Joshua."

"There's some logic to that," Stanford agreed. "Maybe we could wing the guy in the leg."

"Then we're agreed if we get the chance?" Groves asked.

Dowless could sense—see—Stanford hesitate, but then the sheriff said, "Yeah."

Dowless could feel his own breathing rate increase, and there was a virtual chorus of the same down the line.

The footsteps slowed, but they didn't stop until a twig underfoot snapped. For what seemed an eternity there was no sound; then again footsteps moved forward. After another seeming eternity, Stanford gave the signal. A dozen flashlights and lanterns came on, but it was ten or fifteen seconds before all beams were on target. Dowless gasped at what he saw. The spotlighted man, dressed in rumpled fatigues, looked emaciated if not cadaverous. He had a full dark beard, and his bushy eyebrows had no break between them, giving the man's dark eyes an exceedingly sinister look. Long hair in wild disarray fell to his shoulders, and leaves and sticks stuck in his hair with cannibal-like decorations. Somewhere between 25 and 30, Dowless would guess, but it was hard to tell. The man looked so small and insignificant against the tree trunks at his back. For reasons he couldn't explain, Dowless felt a moment of pity for the frightened looking creature.

The combined light held, no doubt, because everyone was as startled as Dowless himself. Although the beams had frozen the man in his tracks for a few seconds, he recovered quickly and unslung a fearsome looking weapon from his shoulder.

The kidnapper was well exposed and without cover in the bath of illumination. Groves got off two quick shots with the bark of Stanford's revolver following them up. The shots were ineffective; the range too great for the snub-nosed service revolvers.

As quick as a cat, the fugitive darted behind a tree and aimed his weapon.

Some of the lanterns were still on when a hail of bullets slammed into the rocks. Shards cracked a lens here and there, and Dowless heard a man cry out that he'd been hit. The gun bursts soon ceased, but in their wake came the distressed wailings of an infant.

"Go back and look after the baby," Stanford yelled. "We won't use the radio any more if that's what's upsetting you."

"Get the hell out of here and leave us alone!" a voice

trembling with rage called back. "Do you want me to kill the child a second time? Is that what you want?"

A second time? What did he mean, Dowless wondered.

"We don't want to hurt you or the child," Stanford called back. "Just give us the baby and go. You won't be harmed."

"You must think I'm crazy," the voice, still frenzied, rose in pitch. "I shot down a chopper and now they'll put me in the hospital again. You won't let me go! You're trying to trick me and take my son."

As though Joshua had heard his own name, he calmed for a time, but soon his wails had a frantic, then pleading, quality. Retreating footsteps ran back among the trees. The infant's voice soon had a wavering sound as though someone rocked it back and forth. By degrees, the tiny voice began to calm and then it ceased altogether.

"Maybe he's not as crazy as we think he is," Groves said.

"Either that, or he comes and goes," Stanford said.

"I think we've got a very sick man on our hands," Dowless said, "and our problems have just begun."

As if the voice of fate herself had confirmed those words, an ear-splitting blast made the rock face under their bellies tremble. When the last reverberations of sound had drifted off, a massive orange ball of flame lifted up out of the valley.

CHAPTER IX

The blast shook the gnarled tree against which Necco rested his back. Small dead limbs fell in the aftershock, and he jumped up with the baby still in his arms. He had just rocked it to sleep, and now the very bowels of the god-forsaken earth were rumbling again. It was certain what the sound was: heavy artillery. The Viet Cong and the Viet Minh were assaulting the hill. He had long lost count of how many hills he'd helped defend, and a sense of time itself had forever forsaken him. The reverberations kept assaulting his ears as though they were great augers boring into his brain. He laid the baby down in the leaves and covered his ears with his hands. He pressed his palms flat against his skull, but it didn't help. The sound was captured inside, and it kept gaining volume. He banged his head against the tree until blood dribbled down his nose and still the terrible echo inside his head split into a thousand harmonics and made him cry out.

He slumped to the ground and rolled in his agony until his body had nested against the child's. He was only vaguely aware that the two of them wept together, but how fitting that they should. Before long, the hill would be littered with dismembered bodies, and the very spring branches and rivers would run with blood. But even with the image of the horrors to come, he jumped up wide-eyed and alert. He must defend his country's honor, go forth boldly in the finest soldierly tradition. He reached for his Browning automatic. It would take down more of the enemy in the shortest length of time. But he waited and waited. No gooks appeared across the crest of the mountain. But that was nothing new. On the hills or in the swamps, it didn't matter. They were always back in the shadows, never showing their faces, and he had come to believe that their slanted eyes and yellow faces wore a perpetual smile.

"Come out! Come out! Show yourselves! I can't keep shooting at shadows!" he called.

Still, he saw nothing. Heard nothing. He squeezed the trigger of the rifle and sprayed left to right and right to left until the sounds of the bullets slapping against rock sounded like hailstones. The mountaintop began to light up with a ghostly orange glow, and his body grew inert.

He watched the vast orange ball rise like the morning sun up over the mountain crest. It began to spread like an inflated hot air balloon, and with its expanding diameter the earth was lit more brightly. He looked back at the face of his child and noticed its eyes wide with terror, and its voice dissipated to the level of raspy gaspings. He dropped his weapon and cradled the infant in his arms. He kissed its cheek repeatedly and cupped its tiny skull in the palm of his hand. The silky hair felt strange, yet comforting. Necco's whole body was shaking, now. For the first time, he was conscious of being cold. The baby was still wrapped in his fatigue jacket, and the long sleeved shirt that Necco wore was getting thin against the chilly air.

He looked into the sky again. The great orange ball was dissipating and burning out. After one glance down through the trees to his rear, he saw clearly the pathway by which he'd come. It was a routing he knew well. Many times before he had come to the mountain crest to seek the answers that had successfully evaded him. He had sat atop a world hell bent on destroying itself, and he had been foolish enough to believe that from so lofty a height he could look down and figure it all out. There was no place to hide, of course. Even here, men and machines sought him out to take his brain, his heart, and his balls away from him once more.

His eyes left the mountain peak, the diminishing orange flame, and came back to the infant's face. There was enough light left in the sky that he could see clearly the tiny ears, the button nose, and puffy little cheeks that were red now from the frosty air. With his cuddling, the baby began to flex its thin pink lips and twist its head to nuzzle against his chest. Incredibly, some strange feeling akin to renewal registered in his senses. Even so, he wanted to deny it. It was a lie, an illusion. All was hopeless and dead, and the whole world rotted and smelled of a terrible stench. Necco felt his eyes spill over with the knowledge. He wished for the sake of the child that it could be different.

"You're already in hell, little friend," he muttered into the child's face. "But I won't leave you, you can count on that."

The orange glow burned out, and it was as though the child's face faded from a movie screen.

"What did they say your name was? Joshua wasn't it? They've just made up a name for you. That's not your real name. You didn't even have a name when I saw you last. . ."

Although the artificial light was gone now, the sky to the east seemed brighter. Necco let his eyes adjust to the moonlight again, and he could still see the pathway at his back.

"Dawn's not many hours away, Joshua. We'll be in for trouble then, so what do you say we hit the trail? Like to go on a combat mission with Corporal Tufarelli? Scratch that. I promise before the angels who brought you to me that I'll never take you on a killing journey. I'll love you and protect you and teach you that the blood of all men and women is precious."

His thoughts and his voice sped on of their own accord until he had relieved himself of a burden.

He unbuttoned the fatigue jacket in which Joshua snuggled and laid him on a leaf bed. Necco put the jacket on, buttoned it a ways, and stuffed the bottom of it under his belt. He lifted the child, placed him face forward against his chest, and buttoned the jacket up to the baby's neck. With his bandana handkerchief, he fashioned a scarf to cover Joshua's head and ears.

"Now, do you think you can ride okay in reverse papoose style?"

The act of bundling Joshua afforded Necco some paternal instinct he had never felt before. But that too was an illusion. His instincts were as jumbled as his thoughts, and his tired and erratic brain was not to be trusted.

He picked up his extra ammunition from the base of the tree, stuffed it into his pockets, and slung the Browning across one shoulder, and the M-16 across the other. In spite of the weight, he dare not leave them behind. The Viet Cong would soon be close on his tail, and if necessary, he would fight to the death to protect the honor of his country and the life of his son. Taking care not to make loud noises, he stepped from rock to rock until he could find bare ground. The moon was unbelievably bright, or was it that this new mission had once more brought his senses to a sharpness beyond the ability of ordinary men? At ground level, and against the skyline, he watched for landmarks that pointed him back toward his home. Strange that he had never thought of it as just a cave. He had thought of it as his home.

When he was well down the path, he had no hesitancy in speaking out, and he said, "I'm getting hungry and thirsty. How about you, Joshua?"

He couldn't tell whether the infant was sleeping or not, but no sound was coming from him. The warmth of his tiny body felt like a fresh loaf of oven-baked bread against his chest.

"You must be getting hungry and thirsty, too, but I don't have much to feed you. I got a little can of condensed milk; would that do it? I don't reckon you can drink out of a cup, though, and I sure don't have any bottles with nipples."

The sky was getting lighter still when he approached the mouth of the cave. The "M" of its opening looked like the letter of the alphabet colored in with blank ink. Necco stepped into the forbidding darkness, then paused long enough to strike a match against the cave wall. The flame lived until he had reached his lantern, and soon the rustic interior was alive with warm light. He shed and stacked his weapons, then began to unbutton his jacket. With the garment unfastened halfway down his chest, the sleeping infant began to fall out as though he—Necco—were physically birthing the child. With exaggerated care, he laid Joshua on the sleeping mat and started to cover him with the blanket. The odor about the child was more offensive than ever, and he unsnapped the pins and peeled the gummy, saturated diaper away. The sight rankled his stomach for a moment, but he recovered and dampened his bandana handkerchief with water to complete the task of cleaning the boy. He stared with wonder at the example of manhood in miniature. It startled him to think that he himself had once looked like that. Just as there had been renewal upon the mountain peak, there was some kind of uplifting in the experience, as though he saw himself white and pure and infantile and thus enabled by nature to start over—to live again.

Although he'd been as gentle as possible, the cleaning action angered the child. The little boy's bottom was raw, the red steaks of inflammation extending down his inner thighs and up his little belly. He had no first aid kit. It wasn't that he hadn't thought of one in his more lucid moments, but the truth was, should he have been fortunate enough to receive wounds either minor or fatal, he had a tremendous need to bleed and suffer.

All he could find that might be applicable was cooking oil. He applied it generously to the irritated flesh, and the loud protests that he had invited with the cleaning seemed to subside somewhat. The crying tapered off to a whimper, but even this low noise sounded eerie dancing about the cave walls.

Necco soon remembered that he had earlier felt blood on the baby's upper back, and that he had tried to stem the flow by ripping away a strip of his tee shirt, and in the near darkness, fashioned a crude wraparound bandage. With the ease of handling flat glass, he turned the infant over onto his stomach. The bandage had slipped

99

downward, but the blood had coagulated nicely. Four small wounds just below the right shoulder were visible as though the child had taken a charge of buckshot. He debated the wisdom of using cooking oil as a disinfectant. He wiped the dried blood from the skin and pondered. He wanted a joint, now, so badly, but instead, he placed a large wad of chewing tobacco into his mouth. Time and again while a child and as a teenager, Necco had seen his father and his grandfather, and other men, use ambeer as a disinfectant. When his teeth had ground the tobacco leaves sufficiently, he spat out a stream of brown liquid and worked it into the four perforations. Joshua's rebellious squawls told Necco that the homespun medicine was working.

Not until Necco had scrubbed off the smeared and encrusted shit covering the infant's lower back and buttocks did he see four more perforations. These wounds were less severe than the upper wounds. He reached for the filthy diaper and on close inspection saw the same pattern of perforations penetrating the diaper itself.

He rinsed out the bandana and finished his cleaning job. Again, he sent a squirt of ambeer into the wounds in the left hip, and Joshua's protesting voice reached new heights. He pulled the child's shirt back down along his body but left his bottom bare. He'd have to wash and dry the diaper later; that would take some kind of courage which he'd never been called upon to summons before.

Joshua's cries were a long time leveling off. The tobacco juice must have burned deep, but that only meant it was doing its job well. Necco still wanted a joint worse than ever, but he knew it would have to wait. He unsnapped his cartridge belt, threw his empty canteen aside. He poured himself a cup of water and wondered how best he could get the liquid down the infant's throat. He reached for a spoon and sat down with his cup at Joshua's head. Straddle-legged, he propped Joshua against his thigh and tried dribbling water off the teaspoon into the infant's mouth. Experiencing the very first dribbles of moisture, Joshua worked his lips cooperatively. On the second try, Necco held the child's lower lip out with one hand while filling the created reservoir with the other. On the third try, Necco overdid it and Joshua coughed it all back into his face. Necco laughed but it was so spontaneous and unconscious that his own sound startled him. No such expression had exited his lips for so long that he couldn't remember when. So startled was he, in fact, that momentarily he forgot the task at hand. When he looked down again, Joshua's pink lips were working one against the other as though he begged for more.

"How about some milk, little man? That sound better to you?"

Necco got up and opened the small can. It was really his coffee cream—he hated the powdered stuff—but he was never able to use a full can anyway. It always spoiled before he had used a fourth of it.

Joshua took the thickish condensed milk as readily as he'd taken the water, but after a time his cherubic face took on small contortions as though he knew someone was shortchanging him. Even so, getting the child to take liquid was a minor miracle, and Necco knew it. Long ago, before he'd gone off to war, he'd spent time with his sister and her child. His niece had required days on end with a switch from the bottle to acceptance of liquid in a teaspoon. Only Joshua's severe hunger and thirst had probably prompted him to be cooperative. He needed a joint. Reality was coming back in much stronger doses than he could take. He had another deep swallow of water, but he held off on the food.

He worked at rolling a joint and noticed that his hands were shaking badly. He cursed his clumsiness and kept up the task until successful. Only after he'd taken three or four deep drags did he begin to level out. Joshua began to look as content as Necco himself was feeling. Before the joint was smoked all the way down, Joshua had drifted off, and when Necco stood to grind out the butt in the dirt, he walked over and looked down at the child. The longer he looked, the more he needed a second joint. Something was going wrong. He had seen with his own eyes the marks of the eagle's talons in Joshua's back. Had even seen the small red dots like chicken pox up and down Joshua's back where the baby eagles had pecked ineffectively. So an eagle had, after all, dropped the child into its nest. That couldn't be. The angels themselves had brought the child on a cloud blanket and left it for Necco's keeping. The gift was the evidence of his forgiveness; the mark of his redemption.

The second joint was smoked more slowly; inhaled more deeply. Things were soon coming up right again. Why hadn't he figured it out before? The soldiers on the mountain—the ones who had come for him in the chopper—had stabbed the baby to make it look as though eagle claws had perforated its flesh. Such men were not above trickery. Anything to get the troops back into battle again. They knew—oh, yes, they knew—that without his omen of redemption, he was their slave and that he would go on killing and killing until his blazing weapon was like a mowing machine cutting down tall grass. Hell, no! He wouldn't go. Even by a false name, the child had been lowered through the clouds upon the mountaintop, and it was no drug-dreamed illusion. The child was evidence of himself, and now he lay upon the crude bed of Necco's home; Necco's child.

Necco began to feel unsteady on his feet, and he plopped down on a ledge in the shadows. The low light danced on the child's angelic face. Such beauty. Such peace. Even hope, perhaps. But the very moment Necco thought 'hope,' some tortuous bile bubbled in his stomach and worked its way upward his throat. The vision of Joshua lying sprawled in the crude bed changed from a picture of supreme beauty to one of profound horror. It seemed so long ago, and yet it could have been yesterday for the wound in his soul had not healed and perhaps never would. How could he ever forget.

For better than a week, his army company had travelled though the Mekong Delta, sometimes by land and sometimes by the river. The silhouettes of war were everywhere to be seen. Shell-tattered trees bowed here and there at the fringes of rice fields. Fronds of palms and the greenery of the other trees were streaked where exploding white phosphorus shells had burst, and wherever one looked, the ravages of war had left scars. In contrast, there were days when everything seemed so peaceful and normal. Vietnamese families in sampans drifted along the river, the children leaning over to wave a cheerful greeting, their innocent faces seemingly oblivious to the devastation all around them. Were they friend or enemy? The Viet Cong sympathizers smiled in exactly the same way as those who supported American forces. For the soldier who could forget why he'd come to Nam, it was a beautiful land. Not even Kentucky soil was any richer, and the rice fields and the patchwork of meadows and forest land was like an intricate quilt pieced together by discerning eyes and loving hands. But it was not possible to have beautiful and peaceful thoughts, there, for very long. The river, the river banks, the inland swamps seemed a continuous network of deadly mines and lurking snipers. The very landscape itself played tricks on the mind and senses: a veneer of reality under which millions of ravenous termites gnawed unceasingly. He had wondered, then, whether any previous army had ever been called upon to fight an enemy so often invisible or phantom-like.

After days of skirmishes with the enemy taking deadly tolls, then retreating, his company had fought their way inland to the village of My Lai. He had imagined—as did his entire company—that lurking in the shanties, straw huts, and mud buildings would be the Viet Cong and their sympathizers lying in ambush. Unto this day, he did not know why the black pajama-clad enemy struck such terror in his heart. They were like the devil in disguise. Necco and every man around him had wanted to start firing and never stop until the last one of them had dropped into the dust. To combat the endless dosages of fear and convoluted reality, Necco and many of his fellow combatants had dulled their senses with drugs.

When the battle lines had been formed and the order

to commence firing had been issued, the response was automatic. They were no longer men but machines who raised their weapons and sent a hail of bullets, grenades, and the vomit of flame throwers, into the village. There was so little strength or solidity to most of the buildings that the slap and whine of bullets could not be heard. Crude homes of straw and ancient boards offered no protection to the inhabitants, and structures burned or collapsed in the flash of an eye.

He and a part of his squad had worked their way down a side street. It hadn't mattered whose burst of gunfire had felled a white-whiskered old man, or women in broad-brimmed bamboo hats darting from doorway to doorway. Children peering out of glassless windows fell outward and inward occasionally, deprived of their heads. Proudly, he had carried his own weight in the opponentless battle. At some point, it registered on his dulled senses that the armed enemy had long gone. Nevertheless, like the others, he kept up rapid firing. Off to his right, he had seen a shack that had escaped the ravaging of war. He put a fresh clip in his M-16 and peppered the structure in crisscross patterns. By the time he had reloaded, an ancient looking old woman had come to the doorway and fallen through it. He sent a fresh burst of fire through the opening and charged screaming toward the hovel. Along the way, he held the trigger down and before he could clear the door, two girls—a teenager and one younger—fell bloody and mangled at his feet. With his weapon still blazing, he walked across their bodies to the tune of shattering glass and accompanying screams.

Inside, someone on a crude straw bed attempted to rise and lunge at him. Only after he'd fired did he realize that the figure was clad in a colorful print dress rather than black pajamas. The force of his spitting bullets drove the figure back upon the bed. He heard her dying gasps before he saw her face clearly. She was a young woman, most probably in her 20's, but it was not her face that held his gaze. The barrage of hot lead he'd sent across the room had sliced her belly open as effectively as a butcher with a knife. In her death throes, she turned sideways to face him and an unborn child slid from her ruptured womb and dangled by its umbilical cord over the edge of the bed. Her eyes, the last spark of life fading from them, had bored into him, asking the question, "Why?" until they had glazed over with lifelessness.

He had stood there mesmerized at the sight of rushing blood coloring her bed crimson. He wanted to take her pillow and stuff it in the gaping wound to make the blood stop, but he was powerless to move his arms. Blood began to puddle on the homemade mattress and overflowed until it dripped on the toes of his combat boots. His eyes shifted from his shoes to the dangling infant. Some faint gasping sounds, as though it were a fish long out of water, escaped the infant's throat. When he had seen it slide from its mother's womb, he had thought, "unborn baby," but he himself had birthed it, birthed it with the fire of his weapon just as surely as if he'd taken forceps and reached in and withdrawn it down the birth canal. He looked more closely at the infant, but the covering of blood and slime camouflaged any distinct features. Perhaps some of the blood was the infant's own. The bullets that had freed it from its watery sac undoubtedly had hit a neck vein. Necco did not know then, nor now, why he had slung his rifle, reached for his knife, and severed the umbilical cord. In so doing, he had seen that the infant was a boy. He reached for a corner of the bedspread that was not already saturated with blood and wiped the face of the child. Tiny black eyes stared back at Necco and the mouth hung open as though still gasping for air.

Necco sheathed his knife and picked up the dead infant. It felt as weightless as it was lifeless, and for the first time he let his vision play around the room. His bullets had shattered mirrors and an oil lamp. A dark colored old bureau and a plastic bag full of clothes bore the pock marks of flying lead. Here and there along the wall were photographs of people both old and young.

Kinsmen? He couldn't stand to look at those strange, yet seemingly warm, likenesses any longer. He held the dripping child as straight out from him as possible and walked back across the bodies at the doorway. Once outside, something compelled him to pause and look back. He looked at the faces of the dead girls and then to the child's. His sisters? His aunts?

It was when he had walked down the dirt street that his mind began playing tricks on him. Far down the street he saw an image of ten children lined up—in a triangular arrangement—like tenpins. The child in his arms changed before his eyes into a bowling ball. But try as he might, he could not swing and release the ball. He struggled at the task, but his thumb and forefinger seemed glued into the ball holes. He swung it around and around and around, and it made him drunk and dizzy. When the dizziness finally subsided and some kind of awareness returned, he found himself still with the dead infant in his outstretched arms, standing before his squad leader. For once, the perpetual smirk on the face of Sergeant Donald Burns was absent.

"What the hell do you think you're doing, Corporal?" Burns snapped.

"It's a baby. I birthed it."

"I see what it is. But does this hell hole look like it needs a gynecologist?"

"I think it's dead."

"Do you see any gooks around here that aren't?" Burns' smirk was back.

Necco had looked back into the eyes of his superior—eyes that were at once mirth filled and evil—set in a smiling face that relished the vision of carnage.

"I don't know what to do with it. . .It won't move and my hands are stuck to it."

Burns reached out and slapped the infant from Necco's hands. It hit the ground with a dull thud, and a puff of dust rose, then settled and was absorbed against the moist flesh. Several squadsmen gathered around and some were laughing, but most were somber-faced. A private came over and kicked the tiny corpse as though it were a discarded beer can. Necco couldn't look. In slow motion, his arms had fallen to his sides, but his fingers were still wet and sticky. Palms up, he looked more closely at his trembling hands and before his very eyes, they burst into flame.

He had only the vaguest recollection of Sergeant Burns slapping him repeatedly. The twin torches at the ends of his arms had gone out, but the terrible crimson stain remained. He had bent and scooped up handfuls of dust and sandpapered his hands until they were raw. But the sickening dark red color remained. They had marched out of the village, then, but at every stream and swamp they crossed, Necco paused to try and wash the stain away. Fellow soldiers began to look at him strangely, and still others avoided him when they could. All of them insisted that his hands were free of blemish, but Necco knew otherwise. His palms glowed in the dark and the daylight from his elbows to his fingertips. His hands and forearms looked as though they had been painted with beet juice.

It was not easy to remember what had happened in succeeding days, but his whole outer body had turned the color of beet juice. The next thing he had remembered was a brilliantly white bed in the psychiatric ward of the military hospital in Saigon.

But all that was old history, now. He got up from his place of seating, walked across the cavern floor to the lantern, and held his opened hands to the light. Save for the dirt of the night's activities, they shone back without blemish. But that wasn't all: not only was the blood gone, but the Holy Mother had sent a sign of his redemption as well.

He stood at Joshua's feet and looked down at the infant's serene face. But why had he thought "Joshua"? Others might call him Joshua but he had never been named. Dangling by his umbilical cord across his mother's bed, he had breathed only a few breaths of life.

But now, his miraculous reincarnation made all things new.

For a long time, Necco studied the angelic profile. Then he whispered, "I'll call you Dinh. Maybe when you grow older, I'll change it to a good Italian name. How about Dino Tufarelli? Would you like that?"

The child slept on. Necco debated rolling himself another joint. His stomach growled, and he decided on food instead. Through the cave opening, he could see that dawn was approaching.

CHAPTER X

Not long after the ball of flame had dissipated in the sky, fingers of fire like molten lava were crawling up the mountain. Although trucks at the crash scene had probably kept the trees around the crash site watered down, the explosion and the consequent flying pieces of flaming debris had undoubtedly arched the general area and started small brush fires here and there. The scene looked like a Fourth of July fireworks display, and glowing cannonballs were going in every direction. The engines could take care of any brush fires within the range of their hoses, but beyond that, stopping the spreading inferno would be difficult. From his vantage point on top of the mountain, Dowless could see a trail of fire moving rapidly up a deep gully. No doubt the depression in the earth was an excellent gathering place for winter's leaves and windblown sticks, dead limbs, and sage.

Under the dying light of the incandescent balloon, Stanford had picked up the sight of Joshua's captor taking flight among the trees. From the way the kidnapper hobbled off, and the way he held his forearms against his chest, it was clearly evident that Joshua was stuffed down inside his jacket. Once again, Dowless had seen the two law officers draw their weapons and he had wanted to scream out, "No, don't try it!" but it hadn't been necessary. In frustration, both men lowered their weapons, evidently realizing that even if they aimed for the kidnapper's legs, a richochetting bullet from the side of a tree or from a boulder could injure the child.

Dowless felt no less frustrated than did his counterparts. Joshua's rescue had been so near at hand, but now the first round of the battle to save him had been lost.

To add woe unto woe, a new kind of emergency was upon them.

Stanford was clearly torn between two pressing priorities. His gaze alternated between the scene of the spreading brush fires and that section of the trees to where he had seen the kidnapper retreat.

"Looks like we'll need to divide our forces again," Stanford called out for all to hear.

There were only a dozen of them now, the others having been sent back earlier to aid in the rescue of the helicopter crew. Stanford kept Deputy Groves, Dowless, Terry Binns, and two other Corbin volunteers with him and gave specific instructions to the others.

"You guys hustle on down the mountain and help keep the fire off of us. If that blaze forms a ring and roars up the mountain, we can all kiss ourselves goodbye," Stanford began. "Link up with the crew we sent back to the chopper and do what you can to snuff out that inferno."

"We supposed to do it with our bare hands?" someone in the shadows asked.

"I know you don't have any fire fighting equipment," Stanford said, "but use what you've got around you. Take some of the axes we brought and cut small limbs from pine trees. Use the boughs as whips against the flames. A fire can be beaten out if there's not too much wind behind it."

Stanford elaborated on other effective methods, but before he had finished, Terry Binns called out, "Hey, I can see another bunch of volunteers coming up the mountain. See their lights?" he pointed.

"Thank God," Dowless said.

"Maybe Providence is with us after all," Stanford agreed. "You guys that are heading back down the hill, here's what I want you to do. Rendezvous with this new bunch coming up and take most of them with you to fight the fire. Any in the crowd that are on the town rescue squads, or the mine rescue squads, tell them to come on up here. And one more thing: on the way down, when you run into the extra deputies that are on the way in,

110

tell them to get up here on the double. I'll try reaching various groups by radio, but in case I'm not successful, you'll have to handle the word of mouth communications. Any questions?"

"Looks like to me this is a job for the Forest Service," a volunteer obviously not anxious to breathe smoke complained.

"We'll get them in here as quickly as we can," Stanford said. "Chances are good that Deputy Wheelwright has already sounded the alarm. I'll confirm that, but in any event, it'll be a couple of hours before any of the Forest Service people can get here. Everything we can do to keep the situation under control will aid them."

"Not to mention protecting our own hides a little better," Groves intoned.

"I know I'm not your boss," Stanford said, "and that you're all volunteers, but you don't have to be a genius to see the pickle we're in. I don't know whether Joshua and his kidnapper are hiding out in a hole in the ground or in a cave somewhere on the far side of the mountain, but even so, if the fire spreads, they won't be able to survive the heat and the smoke. We're going to find that hiding place. Just don't let this mountain go up like a torch while we're in the process."

When the draftees moved off, Stanford perched himself on a high peak and began a series of radio transmissions. Dowless did the same, attempting first to reach any members of the mine rescue service volunteers who might be on their way up the mountain. He reached Spider Cornett and thus learned that a sizeable group—including Joe Fremont—were en route.

"You're just in time," Dowless said joyfully. "Tell Joe he's going to be in on the rescue of his baby after all. After the explosion, the fox escaped through the briar patch, but we'll track him down. There'll be paths to his den, and when daylight comes, it'll be like reading a road map."

"I hope the kidnapper's got a strong neck," Spider barked back. "There's a few of us down here that plan to break it, barehanded, and the first two on the list are me and Joe Fremont."

"Just keep your temper, boys," Dowless said. "We don't want any dead heroes. When the kidnapper's surrounded, he'll probably give up. Somethin' funny about him anyway. I'm gettin' the feeling more and more that he's a shell-shocked vet. Just keep cool, and I'll see you on top. Over and out."

Dowless waited until Stanford finished his own transmissions, then said, "Joe Fremont and some of his friends are just down below us. I don't know when they get here whether that's going to be a plus or a minus."

"Then you'll have to help me keep them under control," Stanford said severely. "We don't want anybody going off half cocked, and this situation could get more precarious by the hour. If that kipnapper thinks he's hemmed in by us *and* the fire, and he's as much off his rocker as I think he is, then he might just decide to do away with the child and himself."

Dowless gulped. It was not a resolution to the matter that he had even thought about. Even so, such speculations could not be lightly dismissed.

Within the hour, Spider Cornett, Joe Fremont, and fifteen more from both the mine rescue service teams and the town rescue squad made it to the top. The others in their groups had doubled back and joined the fire fighters. The faces of the new arrivals were dripping with sweat from the climb, but the air had grown surprisingly cold. Wind movement was erratic, and an occasional blast ran along the spine of the mountain. Smoke from the brush fires laid close to the earth and looked like fog moving among the trees. None of the scrubby growth near the mountain top had yet leafed out, and even in the lower plains, foliage had not been underway for long.

Dowless introduced Spider and Joe Fremont to Otto Stanford. Groves already knew most of the men from Corbin, and he went over to offer Joe a sympathetic handshake and to bring him up-to-date on what had transpired here on the mountaintop.

Joe listened patiently without interrupting, but under the lantern light, Dowless could see the younger man's face grow grimmer and angrier. When Groves had finished his summation and Dowless had filled in a few of the gaps, Joe asked calmly, "What's the plan now?"

"We're waiting for some extra deputies to arrive. I've just made radio contact with them, and they should be here in the next 45 minutes. We've only got two service revolvers among us, and as we've already proven to ourselves, they aren't a great deal of help in this kind of situation. Even with the weapons the deputies are bringing, we may still be outgunned," Stanford said.

"Nobody even thought of guns," Dowless said. "We just thought that if we could rescue Joshua from the eagle's nest, we would've done a good night's work. Nobody dreamed we'd find ourselves in a combat situation."

"What do you think?" Joe asked. "Do you think this crazy will harm Joshua?"

Nobody seemed anxious to answer. Finally, Stanford said, "My guess is, that when the kidnapper knows his back's to the wall, he could do just about anything. I don't know how much of a mind the guy's got left, but when the last bit of it snaps, he may not even be aware of what he's doing."

"We'll find a way to get him, Joe," Spider said, "don't you worry about that. I'll take him by myself if I have to."

"If I read it right, you two are buddies," Stanford said, "but this is my county, and I guess I'm running the show now. There won't be any half-assed rescue attempts without my say-so."

Neither Spider nor Joe said anything in rebuttal, but Dowless could see a certain determination in both of their faces. He'd known them for a long time and known them well. Sweet delicious revenge was a part of their heritage; the sap in their veins that gave an extra dimension to their lives and had provided a justification for some of their past deeds.

The flashlight and lantern that Terry Binns had earlier wedged between tree limbs as beacons had begun to die out. Stanford asked some of the new arrivals to replace the units and thus aid the oncoming deputies.

Dowless sidled over to Joe and Spider. As Fremont's next door neighbor, Dowless had come to think of the young man and his pretty young wife as a surrogate son and daughter-in-law. Even so, there was a side of Joe Fremont that was volatile. Maria had tamed him— maybe even, remade him—but there was still a piece of him that would demand a tooth for a tooth. Something in his mountain upbringing had filtered down; had not allowed him to set aside all the vestiges of the self sufficient, avenging pioneer of the wilderness. Spider Cornett was little different. Nobody ever really spoke about it, and the chances were good that few among them could articulate it, but there was a certain code prevailing among the miners and non-miners as well which was understood as the proper way to respond in any given set of circumstances. Both Joe Fremont and Spider Cornett were too quiet all of a sudden, and Dowless interrupted their thoughts.

"I don't guess there's a daddy in the world who wouldn't like to take the kidnapper of his child by the throat and strangle him. But it may not be the way this time. I've got a funny feelin' about this case, and I think the kidnapper doesn't know all together what he's doin'."

"He knows what he's doin' all right," Joe insisted through gritted teeth, "just like a thief who robs a bank thinks he knows what he's doin'."

"If you believe that, then why has he stolen Joshua?" Dowless asked.

"He's probably a fugitive or else he's hidin' drugs or illegal liquor, and you all flushed him out. He plans to use Joshua as a hostage, or at least as a bargainin' chip," Joe answered.

"There's no way the guy would have been up here just accidentally," Spider agreed, "and even if he was just takin' a midnight walk, he wouldn't have been armed with automatic weapons."

114

"I get the feelin' more and more the guy's a shell-shocked vet, and probably he's armed himself in the belief that somebody is still after him," Dowless said. "If my guess is true, we'd better exercise some patience and proceed with caution."

"I don't care what he is," Spider said, "we're goin' to get him. It was me that shooed those eagles over on Joe, and I owe him that."

"That doesn't have anything to do with it anymore," Dowless argued. "Let's just not lose our heads and do somethin' stupid that we'll all come to regret later. Let Stanford and the other deputies handle it. The state police are coming up the Interstate 75 side of the mountain, and they'll all be closin' in on the kidnapper."

"They've got to find him first," Spider quipped.

"Yeah, where's he supposed to be?" Joe said.

"We don't know that yet," Dowless confessed, "but it's most likely somewhere along the west face of the mountain."

"That could give him ten square miles to move around in," Spider said.

"It may not be quite as bad as you think," Dowless said. "Wherever the guy's holed up, he's got to have a water supply and there's probably two or three paths leadin' to his hideout. All we need is a little daylight."

Joe had said all too little, and Dowless could sense and see the desire for revenge growing in him.

"Joe—we've been neighbors and friends and coworkers for a long time. I don't know what you're thinkin' for sure, but if you've got any thoughts of a mountaintop execution with justification of your own, then you'd better forget it. That's what these law officers are for," Dowless warned.

"A man's got to do what he's got to do," Joe's voice gained volume and edge. "Those that don't have a stomach for it can just hold back."

"That doesn't include me," Spider said. "I'm with you and we'll take him by ourselves if you say so."

"You're not listenin' to me," Dowless insisted.

115

"There's somethin' about the old ways that won't do it this time. An eye for an eye don't fit. I keep tellin' you that there's somethin' unusual goin' on. I can't tell you how I know it, but the guy that's got your baby is hurtin' more than any of us."

"You been up here on this mountain too long," Spider said. "The thin air's got into your brains."

"Didn't you hear what Stanford said?" Joe asked. "Joshua's kidnapper could take him and jump off a cliff with him or kill him just for the sheer hell of it. You think I'm goin' to stand back and wait for that to happen? If that's the kind of lily-livered man I am, then I'm no man at all."

"That's not the issue here," Dowless insisted. "We're seein somethin' here we haven't been exposed to before. It's gettin' to be a complicated world; don't you know that? As young as you guys are, you've seen mining change from mules haulin' coal out of the mines to computer controlled machinery. Can't you see that even the business of livin' is changin' just as fast? The way your grandpappies did things don't have any bearin' on how to handle things today."

"Sometimes I think they handled things better than we do," Joe said tersely.

"Amen to that," Spider said.

Dowless plopped down on the flat boulder where Joe and Spider were resting. The moonlight, and the lantern between them, gave the younger men's faces an aged look. Their complexions had a sickly yellow-over-silver look, and the lines in their skin appeared deeply etched. It was just another mountaintop illusion, of course, but Dowless found himself shrinking back from the mirage.

"I don't claim to be any smarter than you guys," Dowless began, "but maybe age has wised me up a little bit. Joe, you were too young to go to Vietnam, and Spider, you were exempted because of your wife and children, but let's just suppose somethin' for a minute. Suppose you both were kids not long out of high school, and you'd never travelled beyond these hills and hollows, and then you were slapped into the army and taken halfway around the world. On top of all that, you're thrown into the midst of battle for month after month in a country and among an enemy totally foreign to your understandin', and I ask you, how well do you think you could bear up under it?"

"What the hell does that have to do with the present situation?" Spider barked.

"Maybe nothin'. Maybe everythin'," Dowless said.

"I get the point," Joe said, "but even if the guy went through somethin' like that and came back here all rattled, it still doesn't give him any excuse to steal a man's kid. Besides, you're just guessin'. He sounds to me more like some druggie that couldn't hack it in the mines and just decided to hole up out here."

"Even if you're right, we've still got to keep our heads and play it cautiously," Dowless insisted.

"I just want Joshua back. If the deputies can get him their way, that's fine," Joe said, "but if they can't, I'll get him my way."

"Somebody owes that guy one, anyway," Spider added. "Maybe somebody will gun him down on the way to jail. Myself, well, I've got a little Hatfield blood on my mother's side. . ."

"And how did the Hatfield and McCoy score come out in the end?" Dowless asked. "Seems to me every time a McCoy shot a Hatfield, a Hatfield turned around and shot a .McCoy, until both families had been pretty well destroyed, and where did it get them?"

"Dowless, you're losin' your nerve in your old age," Joe accused.

"I'd like to think that my nerve or my bravery—if you want to call it that—has been upgraded by the use of my brain and the messages from my heart."

"I think Dowless is tellin' us," Spider scoffed, "that you and me—Joe—are still just a couple of good ole Kentucky rednecks."

"Nothin' of the kind," Dowless said, "but I've lived longer than you two and I see a whole new world comin' on."

For a few more moments, the three of them chewed the fat, but predictably, no one changed the mind of the other. Dowless got up from his place of seating, stretched, and walked away. Deep in his gut he had the feeling that somehow or other the two young men still bent on vengeance would somehow sabotage what could otherwise be a successful rescue operation.

Dowless joined Stanford and Groves, and the three of them walked out upon a ledge overhang. The deputies came into view at last, moonbeams bouncing off the polished gun metal slung across multiple backs. The wind was persistent now, and far down the mountain, brush fires had spread until long horizontal lines of angry flames could be seen working their way higher and higher. Dowless felt a whiff of smoke. The air had been so pure that this unwelcome invasion caused him to cough. As though his sound was some kind of alarm bell, Stanford called out to the deputies and urged them upward.

When the climbers had reached the pinnacle at last, all eight of them looked like a dirty gorilla band. The weight of their weaponry had taken a toll, and Stanford allowed them a long rest. What little remaining water there was at hand was dispensed to the sweating men, and soon all the canteens were dry.

Before anyone could bemoan the fact that a potential killer lay at their west, a devastating fire rushed toward them from the south and east, and now they had no water to sustain themselves, Stanford started laying out his plan.

"Three of you deputies will go with Deputy Groves and establish a flank to the south. Three more of you join forces with Deputy Chambers and establish a north flank. You other two deputies stay with me and we'll form the center. We'll all sweep with the contour of the mountain and push toward the west. By dawn," Stanford said, "the state police should be coming up the mountain from the west. Don't take any chances and don't shoot unless you have a clear shot and the child is safely removed from the kidnapper."

118

"What about all us volunteers?" Dowless said.

"This is a law enforcement matter, now" Stanford said, "so all you guys stay safely to our rear. If the kidnapper breaks free of our line, you can tackle him but that's all. Everybody be on the lookout for a source of water or any recently used paths. When we find that evidence, Joshua and his kidnapper won't be far away. I don't have to tell you that we'd better get the job done in a hurry. If those volunteers can't keep the fire under control until the Forest Service gets here with men and equipment, we may all be roasted marshmallows. Good luck, and let's get going."

The armed columns moved off as instructed. The volunteers formed a long line well behind them. Dowless was as tired and hungry as all the rest of the early arrivals, but he did his best to keep in stride beside Spider and Joe. Perhaps it was only his sixth sense, but he felt a need to keep them under his scrutiny, to be a calming influence over the sometimes ill-advised courage of youth.

As the combined force got well strung out along the mountain crest, dawn began to break. The view was eerie but beautiful. The rising mountain peaks against the eastern horizon looked like numberless pyramids growing from earth's floor. Clouds of smoke from the fire gave the momentary illusion that the pyramids were really teepees, and that the puffs of smoke might be coming from Indian fires. The men now scattered along the crown of the mountain looked like warriors headed out for a great battle. Dowless chuckled to himself. Perhaps Spider was right, maybe the thin mountain air and the lofty perch had scrambled his brain after all.

The faintest rim of the sun made its appearance, and shortly thereafter, Dowless saw two U.S. Forest Service helicopters approaching from the west. The mountain peak was now between the search force and the onrushing flames. Dowless could tell, however, that the fire was raging more than ever from the volume of smoke that drifted into the sky. When the vast buckets of water were emptied from beneath the choppers, he wondered how much of a difference it could really make: it would be like spitting twice into a roaring bonfire. He was not as comforted by the sight as he otherwise might have been. The thought occurred to him that the appearance of two choppers might further unnerve Joshua's captor.

The air that had been so pure was now infiltrated with so much smoke that it irritated the eyes and throat. Dowless hoped that the Forest Service crews were not far behind the water-dumping helicopters. Undoubtedly, Stanford was wondering the same thing as Dowless saw him attempt a radio transmission. The peak of the mountain was now between Stanford and his deputy down along the highway. The sheriff stood on a high rock and tried repeatedly, but as Dowless approached him, it was clear that his efforts had been futile. Dowless listened as Stanford switched to the state police band and attempted to make contact with approaching KSP forces. Contact was made but the responding voice was so weak and distorted that no single sentence could be understood. Stanford tried shouting in his own transmitter, "You're just barely coming though. There's probably a lot of rock walls between us, so we'd better hold up trying to make contact again until we're closer together. Over and out."

"I couldn't hear much of the reception," Dowless said, "but I take it the KSP boys have arrived on the scene?"

"Yeah, but they sound like they're a continent away," Stanford growled.

Spider and Joe hung back a little, and Dowless motioned them forward.

"The sheriff has just made garbled contact with the state police," Dowless offered comfortingly.

"It won't be long, now, until the circle will be forming," Stanford added. "I know the waiting and all of the complications are tough on you, Mr. Fremont, but maybe the ball game is about over."

"Joshua hasn't had anything to eat or drink now for over 15 hours. That's what's worryin' me the most," Joe said.

"You don't know that for sure," Dowless said. "Wherever the kidnapper took Joshua to, maybe he at least gave him some water. Maybe, even a few swallows of milk."

"That's a laugh," Spider said. "You see any cows wanderin' around this mountain?"

"Well, there's got to be water around here, or the kidnapper himself couldn't survive," Stanford said.

"That doesn't mean the bastard had heart enough to give the baby any," Spider insisted.

"Even if he had the heart," Joe said, "he'd never get Joshua to take any liquid. Everybody keeps forgettin' that he's only three weeks old. He wouldn't take anything but the nipple . . ."

Both Dowless and Stanford saw simultaneously that Joe had lost the ability to speak any more. Stanford pocketed his radio and said, "Let's get moving. The hideout can't be far from here, and when the sunlight breaks for real, if we keep our eyes open, we'll soon be seeing a lot of signs."

Even though walking down the mountain instead of up was a great relief, Dowless was wearier than he'd ever been thoughout his life. Although various mine disasters had assaulted his emotions with greater force, nothing like the present situation had ever tested his physical prowess to such a degree.

The sun had not yet cleared the horizon to the east when Stanford's column found themselves funneled into a carved out swag in the moutain face. The terrain looked as though in eons past that such a cloudburst had been dumped from the heavens that the downrushing water had taken dirt, trees, and rocks along with the tide in one fell swoop. For Dowless, the cleared depression was the path of least resistance, and he followed it. Spider and Joe kept to the high ground at his right with the armed column and the other volunteers spread equally left and right.

Dowless' walkway turned into a regular gully the farther down he walked, and the underbrush got thicker.

Various birds were now celebrating the arrival of another day, and here and there gray squirrels ran up and down tree trunks until aware of the intruders, and then they scampered to safety. The smell of smoke was not so pronounced now, and far off the sky was clear and colored in dull blue. An eagle—or a monstrous hawk—he couldn't tell which in flight—was winging its way in toward the mountain peak, and he realized that even the animal and bird kingdoms were now threatened. Even if the fire flighters could keep the flames from reaching the mountain crest and crossing over, the heat and dense smoke would drive them off, and their deserted young would either starve or be suffocated.

"Hey! I found something," a voice off to Dowless' left called out.

Dowless relayed the word to Spider and Joe, and the three of them hustled toward the direction of the discovery. When all three arrived on the scene, Stanford and two of his deputies stood around a small puddle of water. A few more volunteers arrived, and everybody looked for tracks or some sign of usage of the water, but no one could find anything.

"It's probably just a wet weather spring," one of the deputies said.

Dowless could only agree. The mountains of Kentucky were replete with wet weather springs—a temporary source of water that usually resulted from melting snow or earlier downpours and were productive only for a short length of time. What they all were really looking for was a permanent source of water, and then Joshua and his kidnapper would not be far away. And neither would the spring likely be a voluminous one. Bold springs so high up on the mountain were extremely rare. After the collective disappointment had passed, they all started to string out once more.

Before everyone was in position again, Dowless heard Stanford's radio come to life.

"Groves to Stanford. Do you read me? Groves to Stanford. Do you read me? Over."

"I read you. Go ahead."

"Our column found something interesting. Swing over this way. There are either water carriers or moonshiners in the area, I don't know which. We've found a plastic jug split down the side. I think we're gettin' close. Over."

"I read you loud and clear. We're on our way."

Those nearest Stanford had heard the transmission for themselves, but word of mouth went down the line.

When everybody closed on Groves' location, the whole terrain looked a little more tame. Contrary to what was true up above the frost line, the trees had begun to leaf out, and a few wild blooming bushes broke the monotony of green. A boat-shaped strip of land lay between two ridges as though in times passed it had served as a gathering place for eroding soil. Wild grass grew here and there atop the rich dirt, and it was here that Groves and his squad stood in a circle inspecting the discarded plastic jug.

The object was passed about as though a diamond had just been found. The jug was exceedingly thin, and it appeared to be a ½ gallon-size milk container. Perhaps it had been used to carry water, but after repeated usage, it eventually split at the seam.

Stanford didn't linger long over the find.

"Where there's a container, there's got to be either water or shine. And even if it's shine, there's got to be water nearby. Spread out and look for a spring—and it may be only a trickle—and look closely for tracks."

A new wave of enthusiasm surged through lawmen and volunteers alike, and Dowless felt the surge of adrenalin give new strength. Hardly more than an arm's distance from each other, the combined force started making a sweep. In the midst of the search, concentration was interrupted by the sound of a helicopter. The aircraft eased slowly around the south rim of the mountain as though searching for the sign of life below. Dowless saw the military markings and recognized the big Huey as the same kind of aircraft that had earlier been shot down.

Stanford wasted no time and reached for his radio.

"Sheriff Otto Stanford to Huey. Do you read me? Sheriff Otto Stanford to Huey. Are you looking for us? Over."

"We read you, Sheriff. This is Lieutenant Bedwell. I hear you're looking for *us*. Over."

"Yeah. Wasn't sure you'd come after I'd radioed in last night. Sorry we lost your buddies and your machine. Any word on them?"

"As of an hour ago, they were still hanging on. I think they're going to make it. What can we do for you?"

"Do you see any movement along the mountainside? We're looking for a man carrying a baby. He may be holed up, or he may be on the run. Do you see anything?"

"Negative. You do have another force coming up the mountain to your west."

"That would be the KSP. We're trying to encircle the area. If you don't see anything, you can't do much for us right now. I suggest that you stand by. Your presence may spook our fugitive. Besides, we don't want to be responsible for getting a second aircraft shot down. This guy means business, and he's got the firepower to do some damage if you're within his range," Stanford warned.

"I read you loud and clear. While we're standing by, we've been asked to assist the Forest Service. Their choppers are busy dumping water, and they need a spotter. They still don't have the inferno under control, and within the hour a tongue of fire will be coming around the south end of the mountain. You'd better get your business finished up in a hurry."

"How's the wind up there? We figured things would calm down when daylight came."

"Negative. A stiff breeze is coming in from the northeast. You haven't felt it down there yet, and let's hope you won't. If it picks up velocity, you'll see fire jumping from treetop to treetop, and if you've never seen that awesome sight before, you're in for the scare of your life. I can see entire groves of pine trees and hemlocks going up like oil-saturated torches. Hang in there, and let me know when we can assist you. Over and out."

"Thanks," Stanford said with a gulp. "We'll call you if we need you. Don't wander too far away. Over and out."

Stanford pocketed his radio but paused for a moment before moving off to join his coworkers. Dowless watched the sheriff look toward the treetops. It was a check Dowless had already made. The wind was not yet high on this protected side of the mountain, but he wondered, as quite obviously Stanford did also, if and when wind drafts would come whipping around the end of the mountain, bringing devastation with them.

The sweep got underway again, and it was not long until multiple voices called out, "Over here! Over here!"

The point of interest to which everyone quickly gathered was a small spring that oozed out of the mountain between two clusters of rhododendron bushes. The flow of water was so sparse that it would likely take ten minutes to fill a two gallon bucket. Nevertheless, it was a welcome sight for more than one reason. In turn, everybody soothed his parched throat, and those with canteens filled them.

At first, there appeared to be no tracks and no well-worn path leading away from the spring. On closer examination, however, the routing to the water was found. The user had undoubtedly approached it from the rear over hard ground rather than leaving his footprints in the earth made soft by the overflow. At the rear of the spring, the kidnapper—or somebody—had kept his trail carefully concealed between more rhododendron thickets, then stepped on stones as long as he could. Only when the stones ran out was a well travelled path distinguishable, and here and there an occasional boot print confirmed the evidence. Stanford placed his own shoe over the imprint for a comparison.

"Whoever he is, he's got big feet," Stanford said, chuckling.

Somehow, the implied shoe size and the emaciated looking hermit that Dowless had seen in the glare of multiple flashlights seemed incompatible.

Stanford removed his foot and hitched up his pants. His uniform, particularly his trousers, were so rumpled and dirty and snagged that he bore little resemblance to the spiffy lawman who had ascended the mountain hours earlier. Groves looked little better, and it quickly occurred to Dowless that all of them must now look like a rag-tag mercenary force. The youthful sheriff showed little signs of fatigue, but maybe what Dowless was seeing was enthusiasm for the job which overrode other considerations.

"I think this path will take us where we want to go," Stanford announced to all. "But before we move out, I want to make sure that the KSP are in position to help us complete the circle. Take a five minute breather while I find a good transmission point. If we don't do it right this time, we may never have another chance."

As Stanford moved off, Joe called to him, "If the state police can get a message relayed, tell them to call my wife and tell her that the baby's okay and that I'm okay."

"But we don't know if the baby is . . ." Stanford stopped short.

"Just tell her."

Stanford moved off, shaking his head.

"I'm with you, Joe," Dowless said. "I don't think the kidnapper has hurt Joshua. Somehow or another, your baby means somethin' special to him. Don't ask me how I know that because it's not somethin' I could explain very well."

"Whatever Joshua means to him doesn't count," Joe snapped back. "He's my boy and I want him back, and if I have to wrestle a bear with my own hands to get him . . ."

"And you can count on me to help you," Spider said.

"Let's hope he gives up without a fight," Dowless said. "Maybe in the daylight he's got a little more common sense and knows the jig is up."

Stanford came down from his high perch all smiles. "The KSP are moving into place," he said. "Trooper McLean did mention that if this ever happens again, they want to switch places with us. The whole crew is breathless. I told him that they needed to get out of their patrol cars more often, anyway."

Stanford laughed at his own humor, and his deputies responded with a condescending chuckle.

"You'll want us to keep the same sweep pattern?" Groves asked.

"Yeah, except that you guys on the north and south flanks will turn in and help form a half-moon pattern on my signal. The KSP will complete the circle, and since we'll be in constant radio contact with the state police, you deputies and rescue squadsmen with radios will need to keep them tuned low. I don't know how far down this path the kidnapper's hideout is, but I don't want to spook him with any kind of noise that would give him advance warning. Let's move out, now, and you civilians hang back. I hope a gun fight won't be necessary, but there could be one, and it might get hot and heavy."

"I don't want a single shot fired that would come in twenty feet of my boy," Joe said sternly. "Is that understood?"

"Such matters will have to be my decision," Stanford said just as firmly. "I hear what you're saying, but your son's life is not the only life threatened. Several of us have been shot at several times tonight."

"I couldn't ever face my wife again . . ." Joe began, but let it trail off.

Dowless could see that he wanted to say more, but for the moment he swallowed it.

The path seemed never ending, and its maker had taken every opportunity of concealment along the route. At points the walkway would go directly over a fallen tree, then through a brush thicket, then over protruding rocks until bare ground was unavoidable once more. On soft earth, the path was well worn, and Dowless wondered how long it had been used. There was little doubt in his mind that the fugitive had been hiding out for months, if not years.

The sweep continued through a grove of scrubby looking pine trees, and then beyond them to a shelf of rock. Before anyone had ventured very far across the rock face, Dowless saw Stanford give the halt signal and motion his fellow lawmen back to the tree line. Dowless had not seen what the sheriff saw that had halted him so quickly. Moving to a different vantage point, the explanation became perfectly clear. In the distance—not fifty yards removed—was a deep ravine lined on its high side with a long wall of solid limestone. A ledge overhung the wall as though nature had provided a natural roof. The wall itself looked as though some giant had taken building blocks of stone and stacked them into an intricate and sturdy arrangement. At about the center point of nature's artistry was an "M"-shaped opening passing through the wall. Untampered with, the area would have fit naturally enough into its surroundings, but one thing caught the eye immediately: a well worn path approached the entrance, and besides, someone had stacked layers of rock halfway up the opening as though providing a crude breastwork.

Dowless saw Stanford take shelter behind a brush thicket and reach for his radio. Long after his transmission had ended, he continued to wait. No doubt he waited for the KSP to get closer in and complete the circle. Even so, Dowless could see a tactical problem. The open terrain between the pine grove in which they now took sanctuary and the cave opening beyond would, on approach, leave them exposed. The only way to get to the mouth of the cave behind some kind of protective cover would be to circle the site, come in from behind over the ledge overhang, and at a safe point, drop down to ground.

The sun was not yet high enough to cast bright light against the cave opening. Even so, the stacked rocks in the mouth looked too manmade and undoubtedly had been laid from within. With his heart racing in confirmation, Dowless knew instinctively that the location they had sought was now at hand. No one Dowless could see was moving; everyone seemed fixed with the anticipation of a panther, halted. Dowless turned his vision from the men he could see to the darkened opening of the yawning rock. Save for the chirping of birds and rustling of a rising wind in the trees, all was quiet. A single shaft of sunlight soon filtered between tree limbs and illuminated briefly the point of interest. Dowless lost his breath. For the briefest moment, he was certain that he saw the pewter reflection of a human face back in the cave's interior. Like a reptile raising its head across a fallen log, he saw the muzzle of a gun crawl atop the homemade breastworks and come to rest.

CHAPTER XI

Dowless had been so intent upon what he thought he'd seen that for a moment his eyes would not leave the spot. Stanford was moving forward again, but he hadn't unholstered his weapon. Down the line, bringing in one side of the half-moon-shaped sweep, Groves and one deputy were in view. On the other end of the line, the lawmen were still under tree cover. He tried to get Stanford's attention without yelling. Evidently, from his vantage point, Stanford had not seen the impending threat. With his lips, Dowless tried to make the sound of a night bird as a warning like the Indians used to do. Dowless puckered his lips for a second try, but before his throat would cooperate, an automatic weapon at the mouth of the cave started spitting fire.

Every man in sight huddled behind a rock or retreated to the safety of a tree trunk. The weapon stilled for only a second and began coughing hot lead again. Bullets whined off the rocks and chipped bark from the trees. As though to demonstrate still further his awesome firepower, the kidnapper rested a second weapon atop the breastworks and fired them both in a barrage so devastating that branches of trees started failing like snapped icicles.

When the firing ceased, things got so quiet that Dowless could hear his own heart beat. As frightening as the demonstrated phenomena had been, one thing was clear: again, as on the mountain, the shooter had not intended to kill anyone. Had he so planned, he could have brought down Groves, Stanford, and at least four other men stretched out between them. No, the firing had been purely defensive. No doubt Stanford recognized that fact and Dowless saw the sheriff go to his knees behind a tree and pull out his radio. Dowless wondered if the sheriff was passing the order to his fellow lawmen so that they would give their own demonstration of firepower. Dowless hoped that they wouldn't. It would be the wrong approach and would most likely send the kidnapper into the same kind of frenzy he had demonstrated earlier.

In the lull, Spider and Joe worked themselves up beside Dowless. Both men were awed—he could see it in their eyes—and their breathing was rapid.

"So this is what we're up against?" Joe said.

"It's the same thing we experienced on the mountain," Dowless said calmly. "He didn't try to kill us up there, and he's not tryin' to kill us here. He's just tryin' to scare us off. Make us leave him alone."

"Well, he's not gettin' that wish," Spider said, his courage returning.

Dowless had already thought it, but before Joe could spit out the words, Dowless knew what he was going to say.

"I don't hear Joshua cryin'. With all that ear-splittin' noise, he ought to be awake and cryin'," Joe lamented.

"I expect he's too far back in the cave to be heard," Dowless said, but he was thinking that the poor little fellow had likely cried every drop of moisture from his body.

"Maybe that crazy bastard in there is too cruel to have dripped a drop of water on Joshua's tongue. Maybe he just let our baby die or even suffocated Joshua himself. I want my hands around his throat! I want to get him and get him good," Joe started to lunge from the cover of the trees, and Dowless stopped him only by tackling him around the legs.

"That's not going to help a damn thing, your gettin' yourself killed," Dowless snarled.

"He's right," Spider said. "Let's just bide our time. We'll have our chance."

"You'll both be smart to let the lawmen handle this. Now just settle down and stay out of it," Dowless warned.

Stanford worked himself along the tree line until his view was almost straight into the cave opening. Stanford

131

cupped his hands and held them to his mouth. He yelled. "This is Sheriff Otto Stanford. You're surrounded. Now, throw down your weapons and come out with your hands up."

Again, Dowless saw the muzzle of a weapon crawl atop the stone breastworks. Stanford saw it too and he concealed his body behind a tree. This time the gunman didn't fire wildly at random, but peppered the tree behind which Stanford stood. When the firing stopped, Stanford ventured from behind the tree, and Dowless and those around him could see the gunman daringly exposing himself—at least his shoulders and head—in the constricted opening of the cave.

"That was my answer, and you'll get the same answer next time," the kidnapper called out boldly. "Now, get away from my home and leave Dihn and me alone."

"Who's Dihn?" Stanford called back.

"He's my son. The Holy Mother sent him and the angels delivered him as a sign of my redemption."

"You're not making any sense to me," Stanford said. "Lay down your arms and come out. If we don't get the baby to a doctor soon, he may die."

"Do you hear the child crying in pain?"

"No, but maybe he's too weak to cry. It's been over 15 hours since he's had nourishment. I don't know whether you're sick or crazy, but surely there's enough compassion left in you that you wouldn't cause the death of an innocent child," Stanford pleaded.

"Dihn's been fed and bathed. The Holy Mother commanded it. You don't hear Dihn's voice because I have him way back in the cave."

"If we have to, we'll come in and get him, and if it's over the top of your body, it may just have to be that way, too. Who are you? What's your name?" Stanford asked.

"Corporal Necco Tufarelli. Serial Number 2258813. Name, rank, and serial number. Under the rules of war, that's all I'm required to tell you."

"We're not at war, and the force surrounding you is

not your enemy. Just surrender peaceably," Stanford said.

"I'm not fooled by Viet Cong disguises, and ambushes seem to be your favorite battle tactic."

"I'm speaking in English, aren't I?" Stanford countered. "Are you on dope? All night long when you would talk, you talked like a lunatic. I'm running out of patience. I'll give you just five minutes to think it over."

"And if I don't surrender you'll send a hail of bullets into the cave killing me and Dihn? Is that it?"

"All we want is your surrender. We don't want anyone to get hurt. You or us. Think it over, and don't be long about it."

Stanford worked his way back through the trees to where Dowless, Spider, and Joe took cover. Both frustration and defeat registered on the sheriff's face. For the moment, the kidnapper had the advantage, and with the child as hostage, the lawmen didn't dare storm the cave in a rescue attempt. A single bullet fired into the cave would ricochet and there was no guarantee that it wouldn't come to rest within the body of the child. The sheriff plopped down and expelled a sigh of frustration.

"At least you know his name now," Dowless said.

"Yeah," Stanford grunted.

"And the Holy Mary business implies that he's Catholic," Dowless added.

"He's one of those, huh?" Spider said.

"I've still never heard of him," Stanford said. "Maybe you were right all along. Seems more certain than ever that he's a Viet vet off his nut," Stanford said.

"I didn't understand it all," Joe began, "but who is Dihn that he's talkin' about? You reckon he's kidnapped other kids and has a whole passel of them in his cave."

"I think he meant that he's renamed your child," Dowless said. "All night long he kept repeating the phrase, 'my redemption.' I'm no psychologist but it appears to me that he's lookin' for forgiveness for somethin'," Dowless said.

"Necco Tuffarelli. Dowless, you ever heard that name around Corbin?" Stanford asked.

"No."

"How about you guys?" Stanford asked.

Both Spider and Joe shook their heads.

"Well, I've never heard of him, either," Stanford said. "The name sounds Italian. God help us if the Mafia is coming to eastern Kentucky," Stanford grunted.

"Probably some third generation Wop," Spider said. "We should've never let those foreigners come to the coal fields."

"If you guys got any bright ideas how we can flush a skunk out of his hole, let me know," Stanford said. "I'm going to wait a few minutes until the state troopers get a little closer in, and we'll all have a pow wow as to what's best to do. If Tufarelli didn't have Joshua in there, it would be simple enough. We could shoot him out, smoke him out, and half a dozen other things, but he's got us by the balls and he knows it. We can't do a thing that would threaten the safety of the child. I'm going to move off a way, now, and make some radio contacts."

Hardly had the sheriff passed from view when a handful of volunteers crept up from the rear.

"What's going on?" Terry Binns inquired. "We couldn't hear much of it, but we sure could hear those automatic weapons spittin' fire."

"The kidnapper just identified himself," Dowless said. "His name is Necco Tufarelli. Ever heard of him?"

Terry and the other newcomers all shook their heads negatively.

Everyone was soon speculating a mile a minute, but Dowless noticed that Joe Fremont had grown deadly quiet and contemplative. He knew well what the young father was feeling: all the speculation and guess work in the world wasn't worth a hoot as long as his son remained a captive.

Spider had been listening more than talking. After he'd heard everyone else's ideas, Spider said, "If I was runnin' this show, I'd put a sharpshooter about fifteen yards to our right, and the next time that Wop raised up over that rock wall, I'd put a bullet right between his eyes."

"And if you missed," Dowless reminded, "that slug would go dancing around the cave wall like a drunk bat."

"Then there's another way," Spider took a new tack. "You see that lip of rock overhangin' the cave opening and running on along the outcropping? It looks like a roof projection. A man could crawl along there, and where it slopes down closer to the ground, jump down, sneak back to the cave opening, and grab the muzzle of Tufarelli's gun the first time he stuck it over the wall."

Joe snapped to attention, and his eyes brightened.

This strategy or that strategy started making the rounds again. It was all just one more variation of Monday morning quarterbacking. Dowless had a few opinions of his own, but his explanations were interrupted by what sounded like a muffled clap of thunder in the distance. In just a few moments, a brief wind shook the treetops far above their heads, and with it came the strong aroma of burning pine needles. With the smell, Dowless knew at once what the muffled explosion had been. In a forest fire when flames engulfed a pine tree, the tree literally exploded and sent a wave of burning debris on to the next tree. With the realization, Dowless jumped up and faced the south. His view was obscured by a solid wall of trees, but he really didn't have to see flame to know that it was on the way. Every breath he took seemed more contaminated with the taste and smell of burning resin.

Dowless moved about trying to get a better view. Rising columns of smoke would tell him whether the threat was two miles away or a half a mile away. Before he got any sort of a satisfactory sighting, he heard the sound of a chopper swinging around the bend of the mountain.

As the aircraft came closer and closer, Dowless reached

for his radio. Stanford beat him to the punch and made contact first, and Dowless just listened in.

"How are you guys doing down there?" Lieutenant Bedwell inquired.

"We've got our fugitive surrounded, but he's holed up in a cave," Stanford said. "He's in an excellent defensive position, and he knows it. And I think he has enough weaponry in there to stand off a small army."

"Good luck, but you'd better hustle it up. Your time is running out. The forest fire is raging around the south end of the mountain. It's still two miles from you, but each time the wind comes up, the flames start playing leap frog from tree to tree."

"You really know how to cheer a guy up," Stanford quipped.

"I can't see any of you guys below me. Where are you?"

"We've got our butts behind trees and boulders. The fugitive has opened up on us a couple of times, and this time I think he means business."

"Are you in that rock-lined ravine I can see just down the mountain from me?" Bedwell asked.

"That's us. The fugitive's holed up in a cave and he's stacked rocks in the opening about half of the way up. Got any ideas?"

"Too bad you don't have any canisters of tear gas."

"That might be a good idea if nothing else works, but the kid's father is here, and I don't think he'd hear of it."

"Well, you'd better do something fast. Have you thought about getting the kid's mother up here to make a personal plea? Sometimes even a crazy man will crumble when a woman makes a plea for her child."

"No, I hadn't thought of that, but even if you could pick her up and get back here, I'm afraid while you hovered to lower her in the basket, the kidnapper would shoot you out of the sky. He's knocked one chopper out of the clouds with cool efficiency."

"Then you'll have to do it your way, but don't waste any time. By the way, I can see some uniformed . . . yes, they look like state police climbing up a rock face to the west of your position."

"That's good news," Stanford's voice brightened. "You'd better get out of here now. I can see you through the trees and you're drifting down too close. Don't underestimate Tufarelli. The guy's an expert with his weapons."

"Tufarelli, huh? I married an Italian. They're hot blooded."

"Tell me about it."

Dowless listened while the chopper pilot started a new line of conversation, but a quick burst of rifle fire snuffed out the transmission. Dowless looked toward the cave mouth. Tufarelli had the muzzle of his weapon pointed skyward, firing repeated short bursts.

"Get the hell out of here," Dowless heard Stanford shout in his transmitter to Bedwell. "You're being fired on!"

Dowless heard no "over and out" from the chopper pilot, but the aircraft quickly veered off and out of sight.

When Dowless came back to the low ground where his fellow volunteers took shelter, Tufarelli still stood defiantly behind his wall of rock. His weapon still rested atop the breastworks, but the gunman had stopped firing. Dowless was only vaguely conscious of the men around him, for his eyes would not leave the scene in the distance. He had the weirdest feeling that perhaps Tufarelli *wanted* to be picked off by a sharpshooter. Obviously, he didn't have the guts to shoot himself, but if someone else did it, that outcome would be satisfactory. Having the thought, Dowless chastised himself for wildly imaginative thinking. He was now so hungry and weary that he just wanted to lie down and sleep forever. Only now and then could he capture a breath of fresh air that was devoid of the taste of smoke.

Tufarelli left his weapon astride the stone shelf and disappeared from view. Incredibly, in a matter of moments, the kidnapper reappeared with his captive. He sat the bare bottomed infant on the rock shelf beside his weapon. Joshua's small head bobbled about for a moment until Tufarelli gave him better support. The rising sun now illuminated the cave opening so perfectly that man and child looked like two characters in a puppet show.

Joe, Terry Binns, Spider, and four others moved in closer to Dowless' side.

"Where the hell's the sheriff and his sharpshooter?" Spider said. "They've got a perfect shot at that Wop."

"And Joshua's supposed to do a balancing act on top of the breastworks all by himself?" Dowless scoffed.

"Dowless is right," Joe said. "There's got to be another way."

The very sight of his son had compelled Joe to venture out a little more. Dowless watched him, then called him back. Momentarily, Joe ignored the order and leaned out and around the boulder behind which he had taken cover, as though to get a few inches closer would reestablish the bond between father and son.

Tufarelli saw the movement and reached with his free hand for the weapon. Joe darted back to the treeline, and Tufarelli put the weapon back in place.

Tufarelli started bouncing the baby up and down on his butt with an apparent unconcern for his frailty. Perhaps in the kidnapper's state of mind, he was not even aware of the tender age of the infant. But had the infant been so fragile after all, Dowless thought to himself. The little trooper had survived everything from the eagle's claws to a frosty night in the mountains.

Tufarelli stopped bouncing the child and pulled it backwards against his own chest.

"This is my son, Dihn," Tufarelli called out, using that strange cadence of voice that he had used earlier on the mountaintop. "Dihn loves me and forgives me. I've promised that I'll never leave him. You must understand why I can't let you take him from me. I would kill him—and kill myself—before I'd let you take him from me. Don't you understand? Everything is all right now if you'll just go away and leave us alone."

The threat was so chillingly sincere that Dowless could see its impact register on every man about him.

Joe darted out to the boulder anew, and his quick movement caused Tufarelli to reach again for his weapon.

"Don't shoot," Joe pleaded. "Don't hurt my boy. He's my only child, and Maria—my wife—waited so long for him . . ."

"And I've waited just as long for my son," Tufarelli countered. "I searched for him in the rice paddies, in the swamps, and yes, I walked through hell and he wasn't there. Now, the Holy Mother had mercy on me and delivered him into my keeping."

Tufarelli's movements became more agitated, and he began talking to himself more than to his audience.

"Get back here, Joe," Dowless called low. "Don't get him in a frenzy, or he'll open up on us again."

This time Joe came back obediently, but his eyes had misted and cold fury was etched into his face.

"Why doesn't the sheriff and his men do something . . ." Joe began but choked up.

"He's waitin' for the troopers to get in closer," Dowless comforted. "All of them should be pow-wowing by now, and they'll come up with somethin'."

Simultaneously with trying to anticipate just what plan the sheriff and his fellow lawmen would come up with, Dowless watched the scene at the cave entrance. Tufarelli was still muttering to himself, or to Joshua, but few of his words could be heard. He supported the child with one hand and with the other made Joshua take little "steps" across the stone shelf. The scene was like watching a school girl play with a doll, half imagining, half actualizing human-like movements.

Joe's fury had turned his face a glowing pink. Suddenly Joe called out, "He's too little for that, you bastard. His bones are too soft, and you'll hurt him."

The puppeteer ignored his audience. Then, he "walked" Joshua back across the stone shelf in the opposite direction. As though bored with the activity, the audience, and the view, Tufarelli took the child and retreated into the darkened interior. But one good thing had come from the improvised stage play. Joshua was very much alive and he hadn't cried out in any sort of pain or ravishing hunger. It was hard to believe, but Dowless had the feeling that the child had reached some level of contentment. Mesmerized, Dowless continued to stare and wondered what to expect next. The rifle still lay in place. Would Tufarelli return soon after bedding the child and in a burst of fury start wildly firing his weapon in every direction?

Dowless watched in anticipation for so long that it was like sitting in a theater when the film broke and waiting for the movie to come back on. The stage remained deserted, and Dowless turned his attention back to the men around him. He had chatted for a couple of minutes before he realized something was wrong. Among the faces around him, two were missing. Joe Fremont and Spider Cornett were nowhere to be seen. He asked about the pair, and apparently they had sneaked away so quietly that no one was aware of their going.

Dowless hopped up, and his sixth sense told him that the pair might be up to something foolish. He started looking for them among the trees to the rear, but he could have saved himself the trouble. Off to his far right, he saw them stepping from boulder to boulder around the easternmost rim of the ravine. Not until they had travelled around the semi-circle of rock face was it clear what they had in mind. Then, they paused for a breath— or courage, perhaps—and travelled on.

When the pair came fully into view again, Spider's long legs were soon reaching out for the ledge overhang just above the cave entrance. For a moment, such daring commanded Dowless' respect, but most likely Spider Cornett and Joe Fremont had just walked their last mile.

CHAPTER XII

Stanford came back on the scene with two deputies in tow. One of them packed a fierce looking pump shotgun. He had obviously not seen the two men perched on the ledge across the way, and Dowless pointed. Stanford exploded. "What the hell do they think they're doing?"

"Takin' matters into their own hands, it looks like," Dowless said.

"Why didn't you stop them?"

"They were three-fourths of the way over there before I spotted them," Dowless said.

"That's a nice kettle of fish. Just when we've got a plan worked out to recapture the baby, and now they come along and mess everything up."

"Maybe they'll lose their nerve."

"Fools usually manage to carry out their folly," Stanford scoffed. "That long-legged one has been itching to get in on this since the first moment I met him. I can understand Fremont's lack of judgment when the kid is his and all he wants to do is to get him rescued . . ."

"Spider feels responsible for what happened," Dowless explained. "It was him that chased the eagles off his own place and probably prompted the theft of the child. I know that he's sick in the gut about it."

"That's still not reason enough to interfere with law officers in the pursuit of their duty."

"Maybe we can get them back."

"Didn't I see a radio hanging on his belt?"

"Yeah. A mine rescue service radio."

"Then ring him up and tell him to get his ass back over here," Stanford ordered.

Dowless tried without success, and then it occurred to him: Spider would have cut his radio off rather than chance its coming to life and tipping off Necco Tufarelli that he had visitors just over his head.

"No luck," Dowless said, "they're on silent mode over there."

"I know what they've got planned," Stanford growled, "but it won't work. They're going to slide down to ground and work their way up each side of the wall toward the cave opening. Tufarelli leans out and starts firing again, and one or both of your boys is going to try to grab the muzzle of the gun and drag Tufarelli across the breastworks. That, or just capture the weapon and shoot Tufarelli with his own gun."

"What's *your* plan?"

"In about ten minutes, you're going to see the KSP boys coming up over that ridge behind the ravine. When they draw in closer, some of our crew will act to draw Tufarelli's fire. While he's busy with us, a couple of the state troopers will sneak down on the ledge, and if Tufarelli leans out far enough, they'll shoot him in the back of the head. If that doesn't work, I'm going to call that NG chopper back on the scene, and we'll position the aircraft in such a way that Tufarelli has to lean out of the cave mouth far enough to get a line of sight. He'll lean so far that he won't even suspicion the barrel of a .38 is lining up on the base of his skull."

Dowless felt a certain chill. Stanford spoke as though blowing a man's brains out was little different than cutting off the head of a timber rattler.

"And if that doen't work?" Dowless asked.

"As a last resort, Deputy Grace, here, will try to get our fugitive with a shotgun blast. Bird shot doesn't ricochet so we don't have to worry about the baby. If even half a charge strikes Tufarelli in the face it'll blind him if nothing else. Then we're home free."

Somehow, Dowless felt a sense of loss at the thought of Tufarelli's death or blindness. It all sounded so cold and efficient and inhuman. Still, perhaps there was no other way. The baby's welfare had to come first.

"It sounds like too efficient a plan for me to argue with," Dowless said.

"Except that your boys are about to mess it up. Now, get them away from there before they screw up everything."

"They're not my 'boys' and at your own command, you took things back when the situation became a law enforcement matter," Dowless reminded. "Spider and Joe are friends and coworkers with me at the mine, but I'm not their boss."

Backed down, Stanford assigned one of his own deputies to make the precarious walk around the upper rim of the ravine and bring Spider and Joe back.

The deputy set off with an ill-concealed lack of enthusiasm. When he'd passed out of view, Dowless asked Stanford, "Where's Groves and his squad?"

"They're guarding the entrance to the ravine. If Tufarelli makes a run for it with the baby as a shield, they'll be waiting for him. He won't be expecting anybody that far down, and they can take him by surprise and maybe disable him."

Stanford had predicted accurately, Dowless noticed. Joe had moved along the cave roof to where the overhang was little more than ten feet from ground level. Spider was hanging from a ledge on the opposite side of the cave opening. His drop was considerably greater, and apparently by stretching himself out, he hoped to soften the impact of the long drop.

Dowless watched Joe swing down and get firm footing on the ground, but in the process he dislodged a slab of roof rock which, after impact, generated considerable noise. As though sensing that the noise would invite investigation, Spider dropped to ground also, and with a considerable thud. When Spider straightened himself up and took a few steps to press his own back against the wall, he was limping.

In just a few seconds, Tufarelli was framed again in the cave opening. Apparently, he had heard something but couldn't quite figure out what. He shouldered his weapon in anticipation, but saw nothing to fire at. Only if he leaned far across his breastworks and looked right and left would he be able to see Joe and Spider inching their way along the wall toward him.

Dowless' heart skipped a beat just watching the scene. There was impending disaster written all over the ill-conceived plan, and he feared for the lives of his friends.

Joe and Spider halted their moves along the wall when Tufarelli did poke his head out a way for a cursory examination of the terrain. Seemingly satisfied that he wasn't threatened after all, Tufarelli laid his weapon back on the stone shelf. No sooner had he done it than Tufarelli did a double take. He popped his weapon back to his shoulder and started firing, not down the parallel cave walls but across the floor of the ravine. The deputy Stanford had sent to order Joe and Spider to call off their plan was temporarily exposed along the rim of the ravine. Dowless saw the deputy duck behind some boulders, but Tufarelli kept firing. The fearsome sound of ricocheting bullets caused Dowless, Stanford, and all those around them to take better shelter of their own. Tufarelli kept up his firing.

"He sure does like the sound of that weapon, doesn't he?" Stanford said.

Dowless didn't answer. His heart was in his mouth again. While Tufarelli kept firing, Joe and Spider crept along the side wall even closer. Dowless couldn't tell for certain, but it looked like little more than 18 inches of the gun barrel protruded from the breastworks.

As though to teach a lesson to those who would sneak up on him, and to those who still lurked under the cover of trees and boulders, Tufarelli started spraying hot lead right and left.

Spider reached the mouth of the cave first. When the belching weapon pivoted farthest away from him, Spider sprang into the cave opening. In a flash, he had his right hand around the gun barrel but danced all the while to avoid the whining projectiles coming out of the barrel. Spider pulled the muzzle down toward ground, and while bullets continued to bite the dust, Joe leaped into the fray, and got both hands on the hot, vibrating weapon.

Between the two of them, they began to wrestle the rifle free, but not before they'd half dragged Tufarelli across the breastworks. Although the firearm was pulled from Tufarelli's shoulder, he still managed to keep some of his fingers looped around the trigger guard. With one final effort, they had Tufarelli across the wall up to his waist, and he'd now be forced to let loose, or find himself captive of the two invaders. A short burst of fire once again came from the weapon, and in that same instant when Tufarelli relinquished his grip, Spider fell to the ground holding his bullet-punctured leg.

Dowless didn't hear Spider call out in pain. He stood up from his place of hiding and called out, "Get out of there, quick!"

Stanford and the other men around them joined in the chorus, but Spider was clearly addled. With the captured weapon in one hand and his other looped around Spider's waist to help him, Joe led the retreat.

"They can't run. They aren't going to make it out of there," Stanford shouted.

Dowless knew what Stanford was thinking. Although Tufarelli had disappeared from view, it was certain that he had rushed into the cave to get another weapon.

Stanford reached for his radio. "Listen up, all you deputies give Fremont and Cornett covering fire if necessary. The minute Tufarelli makes his appearance again, splatter the rocks with hot lead. Don't shoot into the cave opening. I repeat: do not shoot into the mouth of the cave."

Stanford hadn't given the order a moment too soon. Joe and Spider had hobbled only a short way to safety along the same wall they'd used on approach. If Tufarelli leaned far enough beyond the breastworks, he could still get them in the back as they retreated. As though he had exactly that same intent upon his mind, Tufarelli was quickly back leaning across the breastworks. As though to test his replacement weapon, he leaned out and fired a short burst that kicked up dust and rock shards scarcely twenty feet from Joe Fremont's heels. Joe rested Spider against the side wall, put the captured weapon to his shoulder, but no fire came from the muzzle. The feeble attempt at self defense didn't matter. In a split second, Dowless' ears were ringing from the various weapons coming to life along the tree line. Shotguns, rifles, and service revolvers kept up the offensive barrage until the smell of cordite predominated over the strong aroma of burning leaves and trees. But even amidst the shower of bullets and shotgun pellets, Tufarelli was not scared away. He returned the fire into the areas from which he could obviously see gun smoke originating, but the maneuver had accomplished one thing: under the covering fire, Joe and Spider had inched along the ravine wall to safety.

Now, things were more complicated than ever, Dowless thought. They had a wounded man on their hands, and Joe's and Spider's efforts had accomplished nothing more than reducing Tufarelli's arsenal by one gun. Somehow, Spider would have to be transported out of the mountains for medical attention.

As though the sound of battle had spurred them onward, Dowless saw a string of uniformed men crown the distant ridge beyond the ravine. Dowless recognized the uniforms of the Kentucky State Police, but in truth he wondered what they could help accomplish when in this particular situation it was not numbers that were needed, but rather, innovation. Necco Tufarelli, Dowless had decided, was no criminal. He was a sick man, disoriented, and given to flights of fantasy that quite obviously overrode any grasp of reality that he possessed. Force would not work. An emotional appeal just might. And even if that worked, there would have to be a touch of the surreal attached to it.

Stanford, starting a radio transmission, interrupted Dowless' thoughts.

"Welcome to the party," Stanford said. "The fire fight's over for the moment, but it wasn't much of a fire fight. We had a couple of civilians get in over their heads,

146

and one of them took a slug in the leg. You guys bring a medic with you?"

A state trooper responded to the transmission, but he had no medic to offer. "We've got a first aid kit but that's the best we can do for you. Your fugitive is still holed up in his cave, I take it?"

"Yup. As crazy as he seems to be, he's got sense enough to know that as long as he stays put, it's going to be hard to get to him," Stanford said.

"Are you ready to try the plan we discussed? I suppose you tried all else?"

"Roger," Stanford said. "I don't like wasting a man either, but I don't think in this case we have any choice. You guys are about 150-200 yards above the ravine. Ease on down and station a man directly above the mouth of the cave. I'll guide you in. If we can get Tufarelli to stick his head out far enough, neutralize him."

"Do you know if the baby's still alive?" the trooper asked.

"He was a little while ago. Tufarelli was playing with the kid like it was a puppet, and he was the puppeteer. I think the guy's completely strung out."

"What's the hurry, then? Maybe there's another way."

"I'm all ears," Stanford said. "I don't like blowing a guy away either, especially a vet that might have had it tough. But the baby's our concern, and while I'm no doctor, that kid is bound to be suffering, especially if he hasn't had any nourishment. If the baby goes into some kind of traumatic shock and dies, then somebody's going to ask us why we weren't in a hurry."

"Are you sure he's a vet?"

"He identified himself as Corporal Necco Tufarelli, and he's wearing military fatigues. Of course, I might add that he looks like a hippie. You know, long hair, full beard, and that drug diet look."

"And you're sure he's not a local man?"

"None of the boys from my county ever heard of him, and no one in the bunch from Corbin knows him either. It's not like we were talkin' about New York or Chicago, you know. He's probably just a drifter that nobody gives a hoot about."

"Very well. When we get into position, why don't you have your forces open up on him again. If he gets carried away and sticks his head out far enough, we'll get him."

"And if that doesn't work, I'm still calling the chopper in," Stanford said. "That chopper drives Tufarelli wild. I don't have to remind you that he's already downed one chopper, and even if we needed any more justification, that little bit of murderous intent is enough to seal his death warrant."

"We read you, Sheriff, but give the guy one more warning: tell him that he either comes out and gives himself up or he's forfeiting his life. We want to do this by the book."

"Roger, but we've delayed long enough. Those gray clouds you see rolling around the end of the mountain aren't bringing in a rain storm. You guys haven't been able to see it well until you popped over the ridge, but there's a forest fire raging to the southeast of us. If we don't hustle it up, we'll all be running back down the mountain toward the interstate with our shirttails on fire."

Dowless looked across the ravine, but Tufarelli was not in view. Maybe the return of the gunfire in his direction had shaken him up a bit. On the other hand, maybe he had gone to some crevice within the cave where weapons more fearsome still were stored. Although the two men had reached a point of safety, Spider would be in intense pain now and probably bleeding profusely. They had retreated in the opposite direction from the way they had begun their ill-fated enterprise and would probably exit at the point where Deputy Groves and his squad maintained a vigil. Dowless told Stanford that he was going to see in what way he could assist the wounded man.

"And if he's hurt as badly as I think he might be," Dowless added, "we may have to get him out of here and to a doctor's office."

"I've never been in a tight situation yet where, if civilians were around, they didn't screw up the works," Stanford growled. "And how do you suggest we get him out of here?"

"We can call in that NG chopper. They can lower the basket, hoist him up, and have him back in Corbin in no time flat."

"We're going to need that chopper, I think. It's going to take something tricky to get Tufarelli to stick his head out of that rock fortress of his. He'll play it cautious; wait and see. I think our own firepower shook him up a little bit."

For long moments, Dowless had been thinking of another plan, but he had held it back for reasons not entirely clear to himself. Maybe the idea was so simple that stated it would sound absurd and cowardly. And maybe, too, Dowless feared that he himself would come off sounding unmanly and appeasing. Even so, the thought had worked its way up his throat and rested on the tip of his tongue.

"I'm just a miner with a little bit of rescue experience to my credit, and a whole lot of livin' behind me," Dowless began, "but I wonder if there's not another way in this situation. If that NG chopper has to take Spider back to Corbin, why don't we let him pick up Maria Fremont and bring her here? Maybe she's the one to make the appeal to Tufarelli."

Hardly had Dowless expressed the thought before Stanford was laughing.

"You think that since a small army of men can't flush Tufarelli out, that some little wisp of a woman can talk him out?" Stanford scoffed.

"Stranger things have happened."

"Well, it won't work this time. The guy's crazy and dangerous. If she even attempted to step out into the open and communicate with him, he'd cut her down and never give it a second thought."

"You're denyin' that the guy has any humanity at all," Dowless said. "I agree that everything we've seen him do demonstrates an irrational man, but maybe there's a flicker of humanity in him."

"If you believe that, you need to go out with me and some of my deputies on a few Saturday nights. I've seen such people as your Corporal Tufarelli choke their own children, hang their own grandmothers, and stick a knife into the belly of their pregnant wives."

"But I feel somethin' different about this man," Dowless insisted. "There's somethin' more complex about this situation than a Saturday night brawl."

"When Tufarelli acts like a man who doesn't give a damn whether he lives or dies, or who he takes with him, why should you be concerned?" Stanford asked.

"The only way I can answer you is this: when a mine caves in on a bunch of guys, we don't ask whether they're black or white, or Baptist or Catholic. We just try to get them out—save their lives. It's the same thing here, but a little more mixed up than that. Everything I've seen tonight convinces me that somethin' beyond your and my understandin' has caved in on the guy. Let's give him one more chance. Let's try a new direction with Maria Fremont leadin' the way."

"Dowless, I think you missed your calling. There's got to be a little bit of preacher in you. But I'm still not convinced. It wouldn't work, and we don't have the time anyway." Stanford paused to sniff the air. "Can't you smell that smoke getting thicker? We're running out of time and you know it."

"That chopper could drop Spider at the clinic, pick up Maria, and have her back here in half an hour. Please? What's a half an hour compared to a man's life?"

Stanford turned away, kicked at a couple of stones, then turned back to Dowless.

"You're hitting below the belt, and you know it. With the fire getting closer, you're not only risking the life of Joe Fremont's kid. You're asking me to risk the lives of everybody present, and by bringing Maria Fremont here, risking her life as well."

"You don't know Maria Fremont as well as I do. She's

my next door neighbor, and when it comes to women, she's one of a kind. The truth is, I think she'd want it this way. I don't think she'd be happy that we took a man's life to get her baby back. Maybe if it was absolutely the only way, she could live with that, but that point should be a certainty beyond any shadow of a doubt."

Stanford kicked at another rock in a fury.

"Damn it, you're complicating things! I'm no hardened lawman without any heart. It's just that this kind of thing is so ordinary. I face it every day, and I long ago learned that you overcome tough situations with an equally tough approach."

"Then mellow a little bit on this one," Dowless begged. Dowless thought Stanford would never speak.

Finally, he said, "Very well. I may come to regret it, but we'll give the plan a try. Now hustle on down there to the mouth of the ravine and get things going. Have that chopper stay out of Tufarelli's range. That's all we'd need. Another chopper shot down, and we'd be right back where we started from."

"You're a good man after all, Sheriff."

"Get going, now," Stanford ordered, "and I'll buzz the KSP boys and let them know the change of plan."

Dowless called to Terry Binns and a couple of the other Corbin volunteers and bade them follow him. In all likelihood, Spider Cornett would have to be carried to a safe site where the chopper crew could retrieve him out of danger of gunfire.

Staying well within the tree line and out of sight of Tufarelli, Dowless and his coworkers headed for the lower end of the ravine. En route, Dowless reached for his radio.

"Ground rescue to NG chopper. Do you read me? Come in Lieutenant Bedwell. Over."

There was no response. Dowless walked on for a few hundred yards. Under any other circumstances, the trek through the woods could have been a restful and joyous experience. It would not be many weeks before the rhododendron and low mountain laurel bushes would be blossoming in a parade of blue, purple, and pink glory. Johnny jumpups were already out, and in patches here and there they carpeted the fertile earth. But the rich smells of the trees and the fertile soil were already inundated by the odor of smoke.

Although Dowless had earlier been bone weary from fatigue and hunger, in the aftermath of the fire fight a surge of adrenalin had given him a second wind. His steps were vigorous and his mind alert. He reached for his radio and tried another transmission.

"I hear you," Lieutenant Bedwell's bass voice came back from the radio.

"This is Dowless Anthony. We need you down here. We've got a man who got shot in the leg. Over."

"Is he in bad shape?"

"I don't know. We haven't gotten to him yet. We're headed to the low end of the ravine. Think you can get in position and lower your basket to us? Over."

"Right now, I'm flying through thick smoke, but I'll find you. You guys are putting your life on the line," Bedwell's voice grew stern. "The fire is coming at you from two directions, now. One leg of it is headed toward the mountain peak, and the other is feeding itself on hemlock groves that point in your direction. You ought to see it from here: when fire hits the thick foliage of those hemlocks, the whole tree explodes and sends a volume of white smoke into the air that looks like a mushroom cloud. If you're all not out of there in the next hour, you might as well kiss yourselves goodbye."

"We may need more time than that," Dowless said calmly. "We've got a no win situation down here, and if we can't break the deadlock, then we may lose the child altogether."

"What's the hold-up? Can't you get a clear shot at the kidnapper, grab the baby and run?"

"That may be the only resolution," Dowless said, "but we'd rather not do that unless we have to."

"Too much humane consideration usually leads to disaster," Bedwell admonished. "It doesn't make sense to save one and lose a dozen. One person is always expendable for the good of the many. I take it you've never been a military man?"

"No," Dowless confessed. "Anyway, we're goin' to try another approach to the problem. After you pick up the wounded man—whose name by the way, is Spider Cornett—he'll show you where Maria Fremont, the baby's mother, lives. After you drop Spider at the clinic, set down and pick up Maria Fremont. Bring her back here and some of us will be waitin' for her. Just so we don't get matters confused, let her down at the same place you pick up Spider Cornett."

"You sure I'm not going to get shot at? My commander may not be too happy about losing two choppers in one day, not to mention a shapely little blonde who's expecting me home for dinner tonight."

"The kidnapper's range and visibility are limited. His hideout is in a cave on the north wall of the ravine. He can't sight in on you if you're behind that line."

"Roger."

"Give us a few more minutes to get in position, and I'll guide you in by radio," Dowless said. "One more thing: why can't those Forest Service choppers dump a few of those big buckets full of water just ahead of the flame and slow things down a little? Even wettin' down the trees and underbrush between the fire and us would give us a little more time."

"They're two steps ahead of you. That's in the plan, but they've really got their hands full. I've never seen a forest fire spread as quickly as this one, but it must be as dry as a tinderbox down there."

"We can vouch for that," Dowless said. "We'll be waitin' for you. Over and out."

When Dowless and his coworkers reached the low end of the ravine, Deputy Groves and a state trooper were already standing over Spider. Joe Fremont paced the ground where his buddy lay like a caged tiger. Dowless saw in Joe's face both anger and a new and deeper fear. Dowless spoke to Joe first and his voice confirmed the depths to which he had been shaken.

153

Spider was in intense pain but still coherent. He had double wounds, one bullet tearing through the calf of his right leg, and still another had taken out a chunk of his skin bone. Shot at such close range, the bullet had torn a massive hole through the calf, and strips of muscle like slivers of raw bacon hung from the wound. The state trooper applied disinfectant which brought a pained cry from Spider's throat, then wrapped the leg in gauze.

While Spider was being attended, Dowless pulled Joe aside and laid out the plan. To Dowless' horror, Joe refused to go along with the plan. The young miner began shaking all over now. The aftershock of the close encounter and the ferocity with which Tufarelli had defended his ground had obviously been a different experience than a Saturday night bar room brawl. For the briefest moment, Joe Fremont had experienced the paralyzing fear of combat and the psychology of war.

Dowless pleaded.

"Do you think I'm crazy!" Joe shot back. "I worship that woman. If one hair of her head got injured, I'd never forgive myself. What can she do anyway? If she gets close enough to that nut to plead with him, he'll just raise his sights and blow her away. That bein' the case, she's got no business bein' here. Forget it!"

"Haven't you ever heard the old adage, 'the hardest criminal will cry at the sound of his mother's name'? That may be the case here. Maria's not his mother, but she's a good example of virtuous womanhood. I don't claim to have any more insight than the rest of you, and the truth is, this whole situation may be causin' me to lose my senses, but it's still worth a try. We simply can't take a man's life unless it's an absolutely last resort. I think Maria would want us to try everything before that happens."

Dowless saw Joe's expression change. The magic words had been, 'Maria would want'.

Joe continued his back and forth pacing, but his breathing had levelled out and his expression grown thoughtful. "Yeah, she'd be like that," he agreed in a moment. "God, I love her so. Just don't let anything happen to her. Promise me that."

"You know I can't make you any promises, but our backs are to the wall now. If we don't bring this thing to a climax, we're all going to be roasted like chestnuts."

It was a bad choice of expressions, and Dowless could see Joe wavering in the agreement. Dowless beat him to the punch.

"I know what you're thinkin', but if it comes down to that, the chopper can get a few of us out of here, and the first passenger will be Maria."

Joe nodded affirmation and went back to his wounded friend.

The chopper was hovering lower before Dowless was fully aware of it. He got on the radio and zeroed the aircraft in. They had no stretcher, but by using a couple of jackets with three men to a side, they improvised a sling and carried Spider toward the lowered basket.

When he was strapped in safely, Dowless said, "Think you can stay conscious long enough to show the pilot where Maria and Joe live? After he drops you, he's going to set down and pick up Maria. She may just prove to be the key in resolvin' this thing.

"You've forgotten that I was buried alive in a mine shaft a few years back," Spider grinned. "If a man can survive the hell of an experience like that, he can live through anything. Sorry I've got to leave you, but I gave it my best shot."

Joe slapped his buddy on the back in acknowledgement and gratitude and stood watching as the basket climbed up to the belly of the chopper.

Everybody started to move off and back in positions, but along the way Joe grabbed Dowless by the arm and brought him to a halt.

"Am I having a nightmare?" Joe asked. "Or is this really happenin'?"

"It's real and you know it," Dowless returned. "But even real life dramas come to an end."

"But am I goin' to lose my wife and baby, both?"

155

"Why don't you just wait here for her?" Dowless stalled.

Dowless walked off. He wouldn't allow himself to speculate on a question too unthinkable to linger over. The truth was, however, he'd already begun to question his own judgment. In trying to save the life of one, had he just been a party in helping to spend the life of two? Or, more?

CHAPTER XIII

Back at base, Dowless found Stanford in the same spot that he'd left him. As command posts went, the site was crude to say the least. On the other hand, the place was so complementary of nature's engineering that Dowless thought of the terrain as a hillbilly version of Stonehenge. That was stretching the point, of course, for the boulders behind which he and the sheriff and others took sanctuary were dwarfs in comparison. But they did have the added advantage of scrubby pine trees and rhodedendron thickets that provided at least a measure of contrast.

Dowless reported that Spider had been loaded aboard the chopper without mishap, and the good news that Forest Service choppers would be dumping water ahead of the raging fire as a cautionary measure. Stanford listened but said nothing. His dour look and stony silence seemed to say that he now regretted giving his permission to bring Maria Fremont to the scene.

Across the ravine, four state troopers had worked their way down the ridge and out across the stone roof over the cavern. One of the officers was poised directly above the cave entrance. There was no way Necco Tufarelli could possibly know it, but if he did not lay down his arms and come out, or if he did not respond to Maria Fremont's pleas upon her arrival, he was not long from death. Not far from death, that was, if he projected his head a mere six inches beyond the stone overhang. Of course, the .38 slug would slam into his skull with such force that he'd never know what hit him.

Everybody in view seemed bored with the waiting. Many of the volunteers growing hungrier and more weary by the minute had congregated at the 'fortress,' and a few of them catnapped.

It seemed to Dowless that everyone resented him for bringing a lull in the action. When the adrenalin was pumping hard, it was only natural that no one wanted the faucet turned off. Further observing Stanford's countenance and behavior, Dowless wondered whether or not the sheriff had bad mouthed him during his absence. Dowless tried to suppress the thought and to make conversation instead.

"Did you give Tufarelli a final warning?"

"I gave him one, but I don't know whether he heard it or not," Stanford said stiffly.

"He hasn't come out again?"

"No, not so we could see him clearly. I think he's hanging back, though, just out of our view."

"We've got to make sure that he hears one final warning."

"Dammit, who's running this show, you or me?"

"I was just thinkin' about what the trooper said—you know, 'by the book.'"

"Maybe I know the books as well as he does," Stanford snapped. "The KSP boys are here at my request and in my county. Don't forget that."

Dowless walked off a way to let the sheriff cool down. Among the volunteers toward whom Dowless walked, Terry Binns alone seemed alert. The wonders of youth, Dowless thought. On Dowless' approach, Terry stood up and asked, "Where's Joe?"

"Joe's still pretty well shaken up. After you guys wandered off, I told him just to hang back and level out. Groves and his men will keep an eye on him. Besides, I want him down at that end of the ravine to wait for Maria."

Terry averted his eyes for a minute, then focused them back on Dowless and said, "That's a long shot, isn't it? Maria, I mean . . ."

"Yeah, it's a long shot, but if we can come out of this with no loss of life at all, it would be icing on the cake, wouldn't it?"

Dowless saw Terry looking him through, and although

he didn't say anything, Dowless sensed that he wanted to say, "But if we lose three when one would have done it, where's the logic in that?"

Finally, Terry did say, "I'm surprised that Joe went for it. He'd be the last person in the world I'd have guessed to okay this plan."

"Yeah, but he knows as well as I do that of all the places in the world Maria wants to be right now is as near to her baby as possible. Besides, I think he agrees with me that there are few men in the world who could resist Maria's sweetness."

"She's some kind of woman all right," Terry agreed. "I've never told anyone else before, but I've got thirty-five dollars in that baby of theirs, so in a manner of speakin', I've got sort of a personal interest."

Dowless chuckled. He'd heard two dozen such confidences in the last fifteen hours or so.

"I'd better get back," Dowless said. "Maybe the sheriff has cooled down by now. I'm not exactly his favorite person right now. He thinks civilians always louse up the works."

"Somethin' better work soon," Terry said. "The smoke's getin' thick enough to cut with a knife."

"Since there's nothin' else all you guys can do, why don't you head on down the mountain toward the interstate? That's your only good exit now, but for your own safety, that's my recommendation."

"Are you crazy? After bein' at it all night, don't you think we want to be around for the showdown?"

It was the kind of answer Dowless could have expected.

As Dowless came near, Stanford leaned across a boulder, eyes firmly fixed to the cave opening.

"See anything?" Dowless asked.

"He's in there. I can see the phantom outline of him. He's watchin' us just like we're watchin' him. And you can bet he knows something is up. The lull is probably driving him nuts."

As though the lull was driving Stanford more nuts

159

than the fugitive, the sheriff ventured forward to the last row of protective trees and called out, "Tufarelli? This is Sheriff Otto Stanford. Throw your weapons out on the ground and come out with your hands up. We don't want to kill you, but if that's the only choice you give us, you're a dead man."

Stanford shrunk back behind the tree trunk and awaited an answer. It was not long in coming. There was a quick burst of fire, and Dowless could see the orange flame of the firing weapon cast flashes of light against the cavern walls. Tufarelli was playing it cautiously. His new battle position was twelve or fifteen feet back from the cave opening. He kept up short bursts of fire, but the sound of it was not quite as fierce as it had been when he'd leaned across the breastworks and opened up with two weapons. Now, the sounds of battle would be bouncing around the cave walls, and little Joshua would be terrified.

When bullets stopped slamming into the tree behind which Stanford stood, the sheriff crouched and ran for the fortress of boulders as though his life hung in the balance. The sheriff, young and agile, had amazed Dowless with his stamina. If he'd tired one iota, it was not evident.

The sun was high enough now that the floor of the ravine was well lighted. It resembled a dry creek bed littered with small stones and a few thistles, wild grass, and thorn bushes. To rush the cave entrance from this side would be a suicide mission, and if Stanford did manage to get his shotgun-toting deputy up close enough to the cave entrance for an effective shot, Dowless didn't know how he planned to do it. The effective range of a shotgun was extremely limited.

Stanford wiped his sweating brow with his forearm and heaved a disgusted sigh.

"The bastard is playing it cagey. I think he's going to hang back and make us come in there and get him."

"Maybe he's not as crazy as we all think he is. At least he's demonstratin' some pretty good battle intuition."

Before they'd finished discussing this observation, a Forest Service helicopter flew over the crown of the mountain and on down toward them. When the chopper pilot got into position and dropped his load of water somewhat to the south, it was only a few moments before they could feel the mist from the water. Momentarily, the air quality was improved, but before long the atmosphere was rich with the odor of smoke again.

A second chopper started to repeat the action. Both Dowless and Stanford were intrigued by this new technology, and again a great sluice of water was falling from the heavens as though a dam had broken. The water hit the earth in a great gush, but no sooner had that sound subsided than another sound was self identifying. Tufarelli had once again ventured out to the breastworks, leaned over, and was firing on the chopper. Dowless saw the chopper swing off, but Tufarelli kept firing. Stanford reached for his radio.

"This may be our last chance. If that trooper doesn't lean over and put a bullet in Tufarelli's head, now, we may never have another chance."

"No!" Dowless laid a restraining hand on Stanford's arm. "You agreed that we'd try it another way first."

"Get your hand off me! I know what I'm doing. We've got to do it now . . . "

"But you promised!"

Stanford made the transmission, and across the way Dowless could see the assigned trooper moving forward across the roof projection. When he came within eight or ten feet of the edge, he went to his knees and crawled. The officer inched forward as unobtrusively as possible, but Tufarelli had stopped firing now. Maybe it was only the smallest pebble, or perhaps it was a larger stone, Dowless couldn't tell, but something apparently rolled off the cave roof, and Tufarelli with a start looked upward. As though he knew exactly what was taking place, Tufarelli withdrew behind his breastworks and disappeared.

This time, he hadn't disappeared for long. His hand

grasped something round and dark. Exposing only his arm beyond the breastworks, he lobbed the object in his hand upward and upon the cave roof. Dowless saw the officer spring to his feet and run frantically to the rear. The tossed object rolled off the roof, and in seconds after hitting the ground, exploded with a resounding roar.

"My God!" Stanford exclaimed. "The guy's got hand grenades. He must have a whole private arsenal in there! What'll he bring out next?"

Tufarelli stayed out of view. Perhaps he had decided to withhold any other surprises he might have for when a final defensive stand became necessary. What if the ex-soldier had a flame thrower and plenty of fuel? Dowless dreaded the thought that the law officers might have to wait until dark, then rush the cave, only to be met by spouting flames that would quickly engulf them.

Another lull set in. Already, it had been fifty minutes since the NG chopper had lifted Spider into the sky and headed for Corbin. What was keeping Lieutenant Bedwell, and why was he so slow in picking up Maria?

To the south, Dowless heard another muted explosion that all of them recognized as another hemlock being engulfed in flames. This time the fallout drifted over them. A shower of tiny cinders floated their way, and with them, the aroma of burning resin.

"That's getting too close for comfort," Stanford said. "With that kind of heat, every gallon of water the Forest Service dropped will dissipate in ten minutes."

"I'm afraid you're right," Dowless agreed. "I wish that our volunteers had some shovels and rakes. Maybe they could create a barrier ring around us that would offer some protection."

"It'd be worth a try," Stanford agreed, "but we're fresh out of rakes and shovels. Maybe you could borrow some from your friend, Tufarelli."

Dowless did a double take. Stanford had picked a devil of a time to start throwing jibes.

"What do you mean, 'my friend'?"

"It's been evident to me for a long time now that you want to save his worthless hide."

"It ought to be obvious to everybody, now, that the guy is sick and not a criminal. The way I got it figured, he's probably a vet that served his country well and couldn't stand up under the strain. If that's true, we owe him something."

"In my business, there's no room for that kind of shitty sentimentality," Stanford snapped.

"Then we live in one hell of a world," Dowless said.

Stanford stomped off, but Dowless turned and walked to the rear to confer with some of the volunteers. The men whose faces he could see clearly didn't look quite as weary as they had earlier. At least the lulls between action had given them all time for rest and quick catnaps. Looking around, Dowless saw that Terry Binns, Arch Neal, and Paul Remy were missing. Dowless inquired of the three and was told that they had decided to scout the area to determine in what direction the fire was moving and how close it really was.

"I was just about to ask you guys that if worse comes to worse, were you rested enough to become fire fighters?"

Vernon Lee, a miner Dowless had known for twenty years, stood, brushed off the seat of his pants, and said, "There's not a man here that won't do his part, but anything we could do would be like spittin' in the wind. We've run out of time and maybe out of luck and you know it. If we're goin' to save our own hides, we'd better be headin' down off the mountain toward the interstate."

A lot of heads were nodding affirmatively, and a low wave of grumbles traversed the group.

"We're not out of time yet," Dowless insisted. "We came to do a job and let's do it."

"Not out of time?" Lee shot back. "We can hear trees blowin' up all around us, and cinders come floating down like sleet, and you say we've still got plenty of time? A feller can't even breathe unless he keeps his nose close to the ground!"

163

"We've all been in worse fixes," Dowless said, "and we've stuck it out—together."

"Look," Lee took a new tack, "we know you don't want to kill that kidnappin' Wop, but I don't think you've got any choice. And as far as shootin' into the cave is concerned, why can't that sharpshooter try to knock him off with hollow point bullets? If the sharpshooter misses, a hollow point will disintegrate before it can ricochet around the cave and kill the kid."

"It may come to that if the sharpshooter brought any hollow points," Dowless agreed, "but a chopper is bringing Maria Fremont to the scene. Maybe she can plead with Tufarelli to free her child, and if he agrees, we can all hustle out of here for a bath and some breakfast."

"That's a fool's bet if I ever heard one," Lee said, and a mumble of agreement went up all around him.

Dowless turned on his heel, but after a few steps doubled back. "When Binns, Neal, and Remy get back, tell them to give me a report immediately. If the fire is starting to encircle us, we can't risk additional lives. You guys can feel free to head off the mountain and save your own skin. We thought it was goin' to be simple enough to rescue an infant from an eagle's nest and now this . . . " Dowless' voice trailed off.

He walked back toward Stanford. The sheriff was pacing back and forth, charged by the energy of anger and frustration.

"What's up?" Dowless ventured.

Stanford shot back a hostile look as though Dowless alone was the source of his problem. Finally, Stanford said, "I've just talked to the state troopers on the radio. They suggest that if and when that NG chopper gets back with Maria that we have him go and pick up some tear gas. If your little plan doesn't work, then we either do something quickly, or we abandon the scene. It doesn't take any genius to figure out that that fire is closing in fast."

"But if we use tear gas and Tufarelli comes flying out of the cave, and we either shoot him or capture him, have

164

you forgotten that Joshua is still in there? Tear gas in the confinement of a cave would either suffocate the child or he'd scream so long in terror that he'd strangle."

"Damn it, is there anything we could do that would satisfy you?" Stanford shouted.

"I know you're frustrated, but it's just that I . . . "

" . . . I know what it is! You civilians always believe that things can be accomplished without anybody getting hurt or killed. It's not that way, believe me. Somebody is still going to have to die before this matter is over!"

Dowless didn't argue the point. Everybody's nerves were growing raw. Perhaps the sheriff was right after all. Finally, Dowless said, "I'm goin' to walk on down to the low end of the ravine and wait with Joe and Groves. If it's your order, I'll tell Lieutenant Bedwell to bring tear gas. I suppose he'll have to fly back to your office to get it?"

"Yeah, and I'll write down what I want him to bring."

Stanford pulled a note pad from his pocket and scribbled hurriedly. Dowless took the sheet of paper and stuffed it into his shirt pocket. His eyes met those of Stanford's.

"It's only a last resort," Stanford said more softly this time, "but it may be our only way."

Stanford had said 'last resort,' and Dowless now wondered what the first resort would be. Just over Stanford's left shoulder, Dowless saw the shotgun-toting deputy sitting behind a boulder with a bored and disgusted look upon his face. Near to him sat a second deputy polishing the lens of the scope mounted on his high-powered rifle. He, too, had the look of impatience upon his face. Dowless looked at both of them and concluded that neither of them had been happy being rousted out of bed in the middle of the night. Clearly, they both just wanted to get the job done and go home. Dowless' eyes wandered back to those of Stanford's.

"You hope you won't have to use the tear gas, don't you?" Dowless accused. "If Tufarelli exposes himself again, you're going to shoot him if you can, aren't you?"

165

"You just go ahead on your little errand," Stanford said, "and let me take care of matters up here."

Dowless trudged off. The bright rays of the sun flooding down into the trees were muted now because of the density of the smoke in the upper air. At certain angles, dust motes rode up and down in the shafts of light. Life went on. In Corbin, people would be preparing to go to work. At the mine, work would go on as usual in spite of the absentee miners who were still captive on the mountain. Dowless wondered and worried about the feathered and furry creatures whose habitat would now be devastated. They, too, would pay the price. Strange, he thought, how one comparatively small incident could mushroom and affect so many lives. *Sow the wind and reap the whirlwind*, he remembered some ancient Biblical phrase.

At the lower end of the ravine, Dowless found Joe Fremont pacing like an expectant father. Joe had somewhat overcome his earlier traumatic experience, and disappointment in himself, only to fall victim to another kind of disquiet. The chopper had now been gone for an hour and twenty minutes, and Groves was apprehensive also. Periodically, Groves coughed a great deal, but Dowless didn't know whether it was caused by the cigarette in Groves' hand or whether or not the odor of burning leaves and melting pine boughs had overcome his lungs. Dowless' own eyes now watered profusely from the invasion of stinging residue, and Joe was similarly affected.

In between coughing spasms, Groves said, "Maybe that chopper pilot has lost our location. Look at those smoke clouds rising above us."

Dowless looked up, and the white clouds were swarming in toward the ravine as though drawn there by some kind of suction nature had provided.

"He'll find us," Dowless said confidently. "When I hear the floppin' wings of that whirlybird, I'll guide him in by radio if I have to."

The calculated expression of confidence brought a brief

smile to Joe's face, but he kept his eyes turned heavenward.

"My men are gettin' jittery," Groves confessed. "They asked me if worse came to worse whether or not we ought not to try the same thing Joe and Spider tried. You know, walk out along the ledge, drop down to the ground, and everybody rush the cave entrance at once. If it worked, we'd kill two birds with one stone. Maybe we could overpower Tufarelli and have a place of sanctuary until the fire passes us by."

"That sounds good if it would work," Dowless agreed. "I wonder, though, which five men want to die first. With any one of the automatic weapons Tufarelli seems to have, he could cut you down like weeds before the first man got to him."

It was clear to Dowless that Groves wasn't anxious to volunteer to lead the charge into the mouth of the cave. Joe contributed little to the conversation and kept his eyes focused mainly on the sky. Dowless could tell the young miner was still shaken from his earlier experience, and still wrestled with the realization that he hadn't been as fearless as he should have been in the attempted rescue of his son. It was a phenomenon Dowless had witnessed many times. On numerous occasions across the years, Dowless had seen brothers, fathers, and the best of friends falter when it came to laying one's life on the line. But at some point the adrenalin stopped pumping, the emotions collapsed, and the mind oftentimes balked. No man could ever know the depth of his own courage until he was sorely tested.

Joe walked off a little way, his eyes focused toward the ground, and his muscular body beginning to wilt by degrees. Dowless could tell that Joe was having trouble ridding himself of the shock of real battle, and the experience of being a witness to Spider's injury. Dowless slapped Joe across the back to convey his own understanding.

"I wasn't as brave back there as I thought I'd be," Joe whispered.

"From my point of view it looked like you gave a pretty good account of yourself . . . "

" . . . I hesitated. I let Spider go first. And it was my kid. I held back 'till Spider had hold of the gun, first."

"Maybe it was just your instinct. Tufarelli's weapon was pointed your way. If you'd rushed in, you might've caught some slugs in the belly."

"No, it wasn't that. I didn't even know which way the rifle was pointed. I was scared as hell and my nerve left me . . . "

Dowless slapped Joe across the back again, but Joe just kept shaking his head as though he couldn't let matters drop.

"It was a lot different than a fist fight after a ball game," Joe mused. "Guess I know now what a taste of real war's like."

"Yeah, I guess it was like that."

"I wonder what kind of a soldier Tufarelli was? I guess it takes guts to look down the gun barrel of an enemy you can't see and don't know. Wonder how many months he served in Nam?"

"It's hard to tell," Dowless said. "Long enough to screw him up."

"You won't mention what I've told you to Maria, will you?"

"No, of course not."

Dowless started to talk about something else when a faint but welcome sound in the distance captured his attention. For several minutes they couldn't see the chopper, but its churning blades soon cut through the smoke clouds. As before, the pilot swung wide and came in out of range of Tufarelli's guns.

Dowless established radio contact and asked Bedwell if he needed ground guidance.

"I can see you," Bedwell replied, "and I've got a little lady with me who can't wait to set foot on the ground."

"What kept you?" Dowless asked.

"In spite of his assurances to you, your friend, Cornett, passed out on me. Had to do a bit of investigation on my own to find the Fremont property. Sorry for the delay."

"How does it look from up there?"

"Dangerous. Extremely dangerous. All you farm boys down there on the ground remember what a pitchfork looks like? There are four prongs of fire heading at you fast."

"But the Forest Service choppers dumped a couple of loads of water around our perimeter," Dowless said. "That ought to slow things for a while."

"Don't count on it," Bedwell said sternly. "With the volume of heat being generated down there now, the trees around you could be dripping wet one minute and dry as a bone five minutes later. Flying around the mountain, I noticed that the fire was slowed for a few moments on Razor Back Ridge. The ridge is kind of a rocky spine that runs from the interstate three quarters of the way up the mountain. Before we passed over, though, a puff of wind came and flames leaped the ridge and swallowed entire tree groves in their fury."

"Is Maria—Mrs. Fremont—terrified?"

"This little lady is as calm as a kitten. She has only one thing on her mind: she wants her baby back and I believe she would wade through all the inferno to get him."

"That's my neighbor, all right," Dowless chuckled.

"From where I sit, I can safely estimate that heavy smoke will hit your area in twenty minutes. I'm sure that you've been smelling it in volume for a long time and getting some ash fallout as well, but you're going to get it for real before long. The flames won't be more than fifteen minutes behind that. You'd better get your job done and get out of there fast."

"Roger, I read you. Will you stay on standby? If our plan is successful, we'll need you to get Maria and the baby out of here in a hurry. If our plan backfires, we'll likely need you to airlift the wounded as well as mother and child."

"I'll be on standby," Bedwell said. "Good luck."

The basket dropped out of the helicopter as though a great flying mammal were giving birth. Halfway down, Maria—in pink slacks and white blouse—waved to her husband. She even carried a shoulder bag. Was there anywhere a woman who would go without her bag, Dowless wondered. Dowless saw the expression on Joe's face turn from one of dejection and gloom to bright expectancy. It was easy to be detracted by the scene, but Dowless turned his attention back to the chopper itself.

"I almost forgot something. Sheriff Stanford wants you to do one more errand for him. He needs tear gas canisters and some accessories. Reach for a pen and I'll give you the list."

Dowless gave directions and called off each item slowly and clearly, but Bedwell was quickly back on the radio with a rebuttal.

"If you want my opinion, I think it's a fool's mission," Bedwell said. "All of you may need me here. Besides, heaving tear gas into that cave might flush out your kidnapper, but the infant will either choke itself to death or cry until it turns blue and suffers heart failure."

"I agree, but Stanford thinks we can flush Tufarelli out quickly enough that we can run in and rescue the baby before anything fatal happens."

"You haven't thought of one thing," Bedwell warned. "What if the guy has a gas mask in there in addition to all his other military equipment? He won't have to come out, and then what about the baby?"

Dowless gulped. Neither had he thought about that possibility. He was tempted on his own authority to defy Stanford's orders, but thinking about it, he knew that he couldn't. He'd been curtly reminded several times that the situation was a law enforcement matter, and Dowless could be accused of obstructing justice. And Lieutenant Bedwell was right on another point also: he might be needed here more than he was needed as errand boy. Even so, Dowless knew that he himself was now nothing more than a soldier in Stanford's little army and thus expected to carry out the commands of his general.

"I wish I could tell you to scuttle the mission," Dowless said, "but it's official business. Just get back as quickly as you can."

"Roger and out."

The basket didn't touch ground before Joe had unsnapped his wife's restraining belt and lifted her clear. The two of them embraced as though it had been years rather than hours since they'd been together. Oddly, it was Joe's eyes that misted, while Maria projected an air of serene confidence.

Even before the basket had climbed all the way up to the rescue hatch, the chopper was swinging away. Dowless watched the skillful maneuver and marvelled at the versatility of the great machine. But machines whether in the air or down deep in the mines were still instruments in the hands of men. More and more throughout the ordeal, he had come to realize that a resolution to the problem would not be the victory of machines over men but rather love over hatred. Even so, would that be enough when one player in the great drama might have passed beyond normal human responsiveness?

CHAPTER XIV

Otto Stanford received Maria with cool courtesy, but Dowless could tell that the sheriff still boiled underneath. Dowless gave his report—that the tear gas canisters had been sent for, and that Lieutenant Bedwell had cautioned that Tufarelli might have a gas mask stowed away in the cave.

"And does Bedwell know more about the situation from up in the air than we know down here?" Stanford snapped.

"It was just an idea that struck him, I guess," Dowless said. "If he's right and we heave tear gas into that cave, it will only be Joshua that suffers. In fact, the child could choke to death on its own vomit."

"Damn it, there's no way Tufarelli could have a gas mask in there. He's a long way from the quartermaster corps."

"And you didn't think he had grenades in there, either, did you?" Dowless couldn't resist.

Stanford charged off to talk with Joe and Maria. The couple had not parted for an instant since Maria had descended from the chopper. She was surprisingly calm, and Joe uncharacteristically agitated and up tight. They sat on the ground with their backs against a protective boulder, and Stanford knelt beside them. Undoubtedly, Stanford was rehearsing Maria on what she could and could not do in the rescue effort.

Dowless took the moment to check with his group of volunteers. Terry Binns, Arch Neal, and Paul Remy had just returned from their exploratory excursion, and all three men were anything but calm.

"We got up high enough on the mountain to see out

pretty good," Terry began his report, "and there are four prongs of fire coming at us."

"I know that already," Dowless said, "the NG chopper pilot brought me up-to-date while he lowered Maria."

"Did he also tell you the upper fingers of fire—near the top of the mountain where the wind is higher—leap gullies with every little gust?"

"Yeah, but we'll make it out. Just hold your breath," Dowless said.

"Maybe we will and maybe we won't," Paul Remy said. "If any two of those prongs of fire run by us and join hands, we're completely surrounded. When that happens, we can kiss ourselves goodbye."

"You're right," Dowless said. "You've all performed above and beyond the call of duty. Now I suggest that you get on off the mountain while you can still make it."

There was a long silence, and every man in sight lowered his head as though he had somehow failed. When Terry Binns faced Dowless again, he said, "There isn't a man, here, who wouldn't stay and fight the fire if we had anything to fight with. But the way this blaze is ragin', breakin' off a pine bough and whipping at it would be like taking a fly swatter to a nest of bumblebees."

"I know that," Dowless agreed. "Just round up everybody you can find and go."

"Some of us have families," Arch Neal added, as though further justification was needed.

"I know that," Dowless said. "You've done a good job—now get going."

"Will Maria be all right?" someone from the far side of the gathering called out.

"The National Guard chopper will be back for her shortly," Dowless assured. "Maybe her personal plea won't make any difference at all, but it was worth a try. The sheriff's getting ready to put her on stage now . . ."

Dowless turned and walked back toward Maria and Joe. En route, he glanced back over his shoulder. To his startled amazement, the small cluster of volunteers were not moving off down the mountain but were following at his heels. Dowless believed that they were willing to risk their own safety because there was something larger at stake. Whether or not they all had a financial investment in Joshua Fremont was quite beside the point; some spiritual bond beyond any man's ability to fully explain permeated the atmosphere.

Maria, Joe, and Stanford stood. Dowless could see that Maria was trembling ever so slightly, now.

"Remember, you've got to speak in a loud, clear voice," Stanford admonished. "Can you do that?"

"Yes, I think so," Maria said in little more than a whisper.

"You'll have to do a lot better than that," Stanford said. Maria raised her voice and repeated the phrase, but it still wouldn't have carried fifteen feet. Dowless had a sinking feeling. Maria simply didn't fit the role of outspoken, arrogant mother, demanding the return of her child, in a voice that was at once bristling and commanding. Dowless looked across the distance to the cave opening. At the least, it was 30-40 yards. If Maria's projection even managed to reach across, her voice would sound like a nightingale with laryngitis.

Stanford anticipated the problem also and suggested that they move a distance to where the tree line jutted out a way toward the ravine floor. The disadvantage of the location was that it didn't look directly into the cave opening, but it would put Maria 20-30 feet closer to the far side.

As they moved off under good cover, Stanford made radio contact with the state troopers to advise them of the latest countdown. Dowless could see the troopers playing it safe within their own cover. Obviously, their near death from Tufarelli's tossed grenade had made them super cautious. If they ventured forth again, no doubt they expected the same kind of greeting. After Stanford pocketed his radio, Dowless said, "I take it you didn't have a shot at Tufarelli while I was gone to get Maria?"

"No, I didn't or we would've chanced it. It would've been over, and we all could've headed home now. Tufarelli's playing it smart. He hasn't stuck his little finger out-of-doors."

The procession through the trees was so solemn that Dowless wondered why he wasn't hearing the accompaniment of muffed drums. He couldn't rid himself of the feeling that indeed they were accompanying a prisoner to his execution. Or should he be thinking "to her execution?"

Arriving at the designated point, Stanford pointed at a scraggly pine tree that was dwarfed in heighth but provided a broad and humped trunk.

"Follow me there," Stanford said.

Joe started to follow also, and Stanford waved him back. "You put on your show; now it's her turn," Stanford growled.

Stanford and Maria crouched and eased forward toward the tree as quietly as possible. Making it safely that far, they paused, then ventured farther to the protection of twin boulders with an air space in between that looked no wider to Dowless than the width of a man's arm. After the briefest pause, Stanford leaned around the right side of the stone and called out, "Tufarelli? This is Sheriff Otto Stanford again. We have a visitor. It's Joshua's mother, and she wants to talk to you. Are you there? Are you listening?"

Stanford's bull dog voice echoed back and forth across the ravine, but he got no response. Stanford repeated himself, and this time he yelled.

Everyone around Dowless was holding his breath, but nothing happened. After the long silence, there was a unified exhaling that sounded like a great bellows. A round of coughing began in the aftermath for the air was heavier than ever with smoke.

Stanford repeated himself a third time, and Dowless could tell that the sheriff had seen something for he dropped out of sight behind the boulder and jerked Maria against him. The quick action had made her lose

175

her shoulder bag, but she retrieved it quickly. Dowless had to chuckle again. Where was the woman, who didn't feel herself naked without her bag?

Stanford and Maria kept low, but from his vantage point, Dowless was at a loss to pinpoint what they saw. He shifted his own position a few feet to the left, looked over the top of a thorn thicket, and then he saw it. It was the muzzle of a weapon snaking across the breastworks so slowly that it actually looked like a reptile. The angle was such that he couldn't see the outline of Tufarelli, but if the moving gun was there, the man was just behind it.

"I see you, Tufarelli. Now answer me," Stanford barked. "Will you talk to Joshua's mother?"

"You think I'm stupid?" Tufarelli screamed back. "You think after so long I'm not wise to Viet Cong tricks? You'll never take us alive."

"We don't want to take you, and you know damn well that we're not the Viet Cong," Stanford called back. "Just listen for a minute—that's all I ask."

There was no reply one way or the other, but Stanford didn't let the silence hang. With a slap on the back, he gave Maria her cue. Maria put her face to the slit in the rocks and called out, "This is Maria Freemont. I'm Joshua's mother. No one wants to hurt you, Mr. Tufarelli—Joe and I just want our baby back. Please listen. I know that he's hurt, and I know he's hungry. Please bring him out to me and let me feed him. Please— if you have any heart at all."

Dowless could hear the impassioned request with reasonable clarity, but Maria's voice didn't even cause an echo. There was no way it had projected across the barren expanse. He wanted to call out to Maria to scream her message, but any call from him would only muddy the water.

In the distance, Dowless saw the muzzle of the rifle spring upward.

"Well, I listened, and I didn't hear anything,"

Tufarelli yelled. "You're trying to trick me again. Here's my answer to you!"

No sooner had the weapon begun to spit fire and lead than Dowless saw everybody hit the dirt. Not a bullet came near, however, because Tufarelli fired on the position from where they had just come, the same location where he had fired on them before. That said something. Tufarelli was obviously so strung out that his judgment was way off. Anyone—and most certainly a soldier—would have pinpointed their new location by the direction the voices came from.

Tufarelli fired his magazine dry, and when the gun disappeared behind the breastworks for reloading, Dowless sprang to the craggy pine tree where Stanford and Maria had first taken sanctuary. The boulder behind which they hid was now only 10-12 feet removed from him, and he called out, "Maria, you've got to scream your message to Tufarelli. Your voice is not carryin' and he can't hear you."

"Why don't you just hang it up, Dowless?" Stanford turned and growled. "It was a lousy idea from the beginning, and now we both know it. I'm getting her out of here before he opens up again."

Stanford turned in a crouch and tried to bring Maria with him. Maria wrestled free and stood up fully exposed and started to repeat her message with all her vocal power. Before she got ten words out, the firing started again.

Stanford turned back and jerked her to the ground. Grabbing her by the hand again, he headed for the cover of trees. The two of them were almost parallel with Dowless when Maria jerked free. Before the sheriff could turn around and figure how and where he'd lost her, Maria was darting back toward the boulder. She stopped there only long enough to pick up her dropped shoulder bag and then ran toward the floor of the ravine. Her speed was too great for the unstable footing of the barren ground, and she took a spill, recovered herself and her shoulder bag quickly, and sprinted ahead. Only now did

Dowless discern the importance of that shoulder bag. It was not a regular shoulder bag: it was her diaper bag, and all along it was now certain that she had plotted precisely the foolish act that she now undertook.

Stanford was no more hypnotized than Dowless himself. Everything had happened so quickly, so unexpectedly, that tired bodies and weary minds were slow to grasp it. Nevertheless, Stanford sprang to action. "Get into positions! We've got to give her cover fire! He'll gun her down when he sees her coming . . ."

Stanford literally shoved his sharpshooting deputy toward an advantageous position for firing.

"You've been itching for the chance," Stanford called after him, "now you've got it. If you get a clear shot, blow his head off."

Dowless could hardly disagree with the order, now. The rules of the game had changed. Ricochetting bullets might still injure the child, but now his mother's life was at stake, too.

As Stanford and his deputies opened up, the sound was deafening. Gun smoke was indistinguishable from the fire fog, and the slap of bullets against the distant rocks and breastworks bounced back with a fearful echo.

Dowless realized that Stanford had not had time to radio the state troopers along the ridge behind the cave, but they, too, had obviously seen all too clearly what had transpired. Four of them were working their way down cautiously toward the cave roof.

Dowless wanted to cheer for Maria. Joe was quickly at his side, but he was too terrified to speak. The girl ran bravely on, though he could tell that she was tiring badly. Soon, she would present her protectors with a dilemma: as she neared the cave opening, cover fire would have to be redirected and therefore less effective. At that point, all that Stanford and his men could do was provide noise.

The state troopers began firing also, directing their barrage into the ground to each side of the cave. Undoubtedly, they thought that their own firepower would be distracting, if not threatening, and with luck, convince the wily Tufarelli that the hail of gun fire meant a quick and imminent invasion of his sanctuary.

Tufarelli kept up a left to right sweep with his weapon until Dowless wondered if the gun barrel was not red hot. The only time he seemed to pause was after the first hail of bullets coming from the troopers over his head. But as before, he was prepared for new visitors in the old location. While still firing with one hand, Tufarelli started lobbing grenades with the other. The troopers ran for cover while the grenades rolled off, and as though his timing was perfect, Tufarelli ducked just long enough for the grenades to explode. The earth-shattering sounds of the miniature bombs exploding brought Maria to a halt momentarily. Dowless stood up and tried to call her back, but there was still too much noise to make himself heard. Joe, too, had recovered his voice and stood screaming demands at his wife that were equally futile.

"Oh, God! She's goin' to die, Dowless. He'll shoot her down like a rabid dog," Joe cried.

"Keep the faith, Joe. Keep the faith," Dowless called back, but it was as though he had said nothing. Joe's tired and dirty face was growing streaked with tears, and his powerful body soon shook with sounds of anguish.

Across the way, the state troopers were moving back toward the ridge. They seemingly realized that their effort would ultimately endanger Maria rather than help her. If Tufarelli kept lobbing his grenades and they kept falling to the ground and exploding, the closer Maria came, the more endangered her life became.

Disasterously, Maria started swinging wide rather than running parallel to the distant ravine wall in which the cave was inset. The action invited Tufarelli to use her own body as a target, and yet Dowless had the strongest sense that her action was not one of foolhardiness but one of calculated design.

As she closed the distance, Stanford called out, "Cease firing! Cease firing!"

Stanford's sharpshooting deputy lowered his rifle reluctantly. Tufarelli's expertly constructed breastworks had obviously not exposed him much below the eyeballs. Even when he'd leaned over to lob a grenade, so quick had been his actions that lining up the rifle's cross hairs rapidly was not an easy thing to accomplish. Nevertheless, Stanford told his sharpshooter to stand ready in the event that Tufarelli reappeared at the breastworks and incautiously exposed himself for even a fatal moment.

Maria took advantage of the lull by picking up speed and heading straight for the cave opening. She was still 12-15 yards short of the breastworks when like a jack-in-the-box, Tufarelli popped up over the wall and started firing again. His bullets peppered the ground to each side of her, raising a circle of miniature dust clouds.

Stanford's sharpshooter raised his weapon, but by the time the dust clouds cleared, Maria's own head was directly in line with that of Tufarelli's.

Bravely, she walked ahead, apparently sensing that her child's kidnapper could have killed her ten times over and had decided, for reasons of his own, not to do so. She reached the breastworks and paused as though asking permission to enter. If that had been her question, and if she awaited an answer, it was not long in coming. A hand reached over the wall and literally dragged her across.

When everyone's breath returned, Dowless saw Stanford's hostile eyes search him out. It seemed to Dowless that the moist eyes of Joe Fremont were no less hostile.

"Well, Dowless, are you satisfied now? In exchange for your intended benevolence to that weirdo over there, we've just handed him another prisoner," Stanford chided.

"I don't guess there's anything for me to say," Dowless lowered his head.

Although each man now kept his tongue, nature didn't. A resounding clap not unlike the crash of thunder resounded, and inquiring eyes saw a pumpkin-shaped hemlock tree on the near ridge explode and turn into a ball of flame.

CHAPTER XV

Maria had looked into the glassy eyes for only the briefest moment before the hairy arm reached for her, pulling her belly down up and over the stone wall. She landed on the cave floor with enough impact to momentarily dull her senses. When she got her wind back, she looked up to see the figure of a man standing over her, gun in hand. The light inside the cave was dim compared to the sun brightened ravine floor. She made no quick moves and gave her eyes a moment to adjust. Slowly, the man's features came into focus, and when they did, she started. His face, his busy eyebrows, his long hair, his beard, the composite reminded her of pictures she'd seen of Charles Manson, the California murderer and hippie leader.

She started to rise, but he raised his foot and placed the sole of his boot against her shoulder and upper chest.

"I want my baby," she pleaded. "I want Joshua."

He withdrew his foot but kept the gun pointed at her. She stood up slowly, and his eyes never left her for a second.

"What have you done with Joshua?" she pleaded anew.

"There's so one here by that name. There's only Dihn and me."

His voice was soft—even a little listless—and she had expected the contrary since earlier she had heard him yelling harshly across the compound to Dowless, Sheriff Stanford, and the others. She had been well briefed in what had transpired up to the moment of her arrival, but the collective information had not really prepared her to stand in the presence of Necco Tufarelli. There was no doubt in her mind that he was strung out, but if

181

he were on uppers, they weren't working. There was a melancholy air about him, and though his eyes penetrated her deeply, they had the quality of seeing her and passing beyond.

"Who is Dihn?"

"He's my son. He's my absolution. The Holy Mother brought him to me."

"Would you show me your son?"

His eyes searched her for a moment as if to determine the sincerity of her request. She was no longer frightened and trembling as she had been upon first looking into his face. Now she discerned a softness in his features, a kindness in his eyes. Still, he somehow hadn't the will or the capacity to smile, and an aura of sadness clung to him.

Tufarelli took a few steps toward the rear of the cave and turned to make sure she was following.

"*They* haven't left us in peace. They've forced me to defend my home, and Dihn has wept until there's no more strength in his voice."

Maria felt her heart stop. Did he mean that Joshua was dead?

"Where have you put Josh . . . Dihn?

He didn't answer and kept on walking. Any rays of sunlight to their rear disappeared, and she began to see the soft glow of lantern light.

"Where have I put my son?" he answered at last. "He's in the palm of my hand and in the hollow of my heart where he'll always be, but in the presence of enemies, I've hidden him well."

Reacting to the possessive hautiness in Tufarelli's tone, Maria replied, "I'm not his enemy, and by whatever name you call him, I'm still his mother."

"You couldn't be. You weren't there, and she was much smaller than you."

"I don't know what you're trying to say. Won't you please take me to my child? I know that he's starving, and maybe he's desperately ill."

The thoughts and fears that had been temporarily

pushed aside in the excitement of the gunfire and danger such as she had never known before, now came hauntingly back.

"But I tried to feed Dihn, though his mouth is so small . . . and he's not happy with what food I have."

The orange light of the lantern grew brighter, and in the middle of the cave floor, a blanket was spread out as bedding. Here and there, protruding ledges held a few utensils and food supplies, but Tufarelli's "home" was unbelievably filthy and primitive. She looked about in the hope of seeing some crudely fashioned infant's bed. She wanted to drop all caution and run and search every nook and cranny within the deep cavern, but something told her an air of calm needed to be maintained. Some instinct said that Necco Tufarelli was a bomb ready to explode, and she exercised rigid control over herself.

Her eyes alighted upon a rock ledge over which was spread a long linen cloth. In spite of herself, a little cry escaped her throat. It was a baby's diaper, drying.

"Take me to Dihn," she pleaded anew. "I know you must love him very much. I see that you've changed his diaper and washed it. There must be a tenderness in you . . ."

As though she had paid him the supreme compliment, a brief though pained smile traversed his face.

"Yes, Dihn's a great gift to me. When I saw you running across the ravine floor, I thought that you were Dihn's mother coming back to be with him. But I knew that couldn't be since I . . . since I . . . and I knew I couldn't shoot you again like the first time . . ."

He was not making any sense at all, but she listened to every jumbled thought, every twisted phrase until he grew silent again.

"Please take me to Dihn," she asked once more.

As though the child himself had heard her, she discerned the faintest whimper somewhere deep in the cavern. But the little voice was so weak and listless, so drained of energy, that it was more of a gurgle than a whimper.

"He sounds too weak to cry," Maria said, and her own eyes had begun to spill over. She had reached the limits of calmness and self control. Tufarelli's measured speech and calculatedly slow movements were having an odd effect upon her, and now she wanted to scream out to break the spell.

"You are toying with me," she accused. "I want my child so I can feed him. I'm running over with milk while he suffers from hunger."

His eyes appraised her with greater scrutiny, and his vision lingered overlong on the fullness of her breasts. She looked down at herself and discovered the wetness her seeping nipples had caused.

"You see? Dihn's nourishment drains away, and you stand there playing games with me. If you truly love him, bring him to me."

A new awareness of her suggested itself in his countenance. He said nothing and moved off, mechanical-like, to a darkened area of the cave. Maria held her breath, and she could feel the seepage of milk trickle down her belly and on down her thighs.

An eternity passed, but he began emerging from the shadows with a bundle in his arms. As he came closer, Maria could see that Joshua was wrapped in a dirty bath towel, and she ran forward to receive him. Tufaelli yielded the infant, but Joshua was limp in her arms. What had happened to the little ball of flesh so charged with energy and so quick to nuzzle at her breast? Now she couldn't hold back the tears. She looked through flooding eyes for a place of seating but saw none.

As though some fatherly instinct was resident in Tufarelli after all, he took her by the arm and led her to a stone bench to the side of his crude sleeping mat. She peeled the dirty towel from around her child's body and saw his angelic face bathed in the soft lantern light. There seemed not enough energy left in him to open his tiny mouth, but with her pleading and cooing, she elicited a response. She let the diaper bag slide from her shoulder and began unbuttoning her blouse. She waited

184

for Tufarelli to move away, but his gaze was transfixed upon her, and he stood his ground. She undid the remaining buttons, lowered the straps of her nursing bra and attempted to force a nipple into Joshua's mouth. With repeated effort, she succeeded, but at first Joshua seemed too weak to suck. She rocked the child back and forth until through some instinctive recognition, his soft lips began working on their own.

Up to now, she had tried hard not to hate Necco Tufarelli. From all that she had learned from the chopper pilot, from Dowless, Joe, and Sheriff Stanford, she had believed him emotionally ill. There was less doubt now of that supposition, but even so, she found it difficult to forgive him for Joshua's hours of unnecessary captivity. Unquestionably, her son had been exposed to so much terror, noise, and interruption of his normal sleep that he had been drained of his strength to the point of coma or death. She lifted her eyes once more to face this perpetrator of terror, but to her surprise, tears dribbled down his cheeks. His vision was firmly fixed on the feeding child, but there was no lust in his eyes at seeing her exposure, only a kind of soft wonder.

As Joshua's sucking became more powerful, she eased the shirt up his back and saw the wound the eagle claws had made. She also saw that someone had attended those wounds, and that they were not as horrendous as she had pictured them. She saw, too, the tiny red specks up and down his back that looked like the blotches of chicken pox. Those would be the beak marks of baby eagles trying to penetrate Joshua's flesh, of course. God had heard her prayers. It was evident now that Joshua's face had been turned toward the outer rim of the nest, and thus his eyes and face had been protected. She had already seen that her child's precious face had suffered no more damage than scratch marks from the sticks and grass from which the nest had been constructed, and she breathed a second prayer of gratitude.

She switched Joshua to the other breast. Every ounce of milk was putting strength back into his tiny body, and when he started rubbing one leg against the other in a kind of joyful undulation, she felt a new sense of well-being.

"He's not Dihn at all," Tufarelli whispered.

"What did you say?"

"I said that he's not Dihn at all. He's your child. Joshua."

"Yes, he is Joshua. We—my husband Joe and I—gave him that name because it means 'whom God has given.' You see, we couldn't have a child, but through the miracle of modern medicine he was born to us."

She found herself giving this stranger—this terrorist— a brief history of the in vitro fertilization she had undergone. Why had she done this, she wondered? What quality in Tufarelli emerged through the uncleanliness of his person and the earlier demonstration of his hostility to elicit this personal information from her?

He asked questions, and after she had answered them, he was more than touched, for now soft sobs escaped his throat. After a moment, he said, "I once killed a child like Joshua, and his mother as well. It was in Viet Nam, and after it happened, the blood on my hands and arms turned to flames. For days afterward, I couldn't wash the blood away. . ."

As she had related her story to him, so he did likewise to her. She wept with him in his anguish, and he wandered away as though to hide his face. She held Joshua all the more tightly to her, then, and as she shifted his body, she saw the second set of talon perforations on his hip. The same streaks of brown medication that Tufarelli had used to disinfect and stop the bleeding feathered out from the wound in erratic patterns. She looked out across the cavern floor and saw Tufaelli leaning against the wall. He held his own head in his hands as though some terrible vibration echoed back and forth between his ears, and he was powerless to stop it.

"It was kind of you to tend Joshua's wounds," she called out.

He didn't hear her for it seemed that the demons that

186

possessed him had closed his ears and gouged out his sight. She repeated herself more loudly, and he turned his attention toward her.

"What did you say?"

"I said that it took a caring person to attend my baby's wounds."

He came back over and pointed at the infant's tiny hip.

"The brown-looking stuff is ambeer. Tobacco juice. It's good disinfectant but it stings and it made Joshua cry."

"But it kept the germs away and that's the important thing."

"But he cried and cried until he couldn't cry any more. I had to shoot back at the Viet. . .at those who wanted to take him from me, and the sounds were so loud in here that I thought I'd killed him. He kept trying to cry, and he couldn't. He was turning blue in the face, and I beathed in his mouth and took him way far back in the cave where it was quieter."

Joshua had sucked her dry. She eased him back along her knees and buttoned her blouse. She laid him on Tufarelli's blanket bed and completed his dressing. While fastening the diaper, her fingers felt the residue of oil, and she paused questioningly.

"It's cooking oil," he said, "I didn't have anything else and he had a real bad rash."

This time she made no comment, but a smile formed on her face in appreciation for his ingenuity. As she completed her task, then looked up, he was starting to roll a joint, and she stared him down. In the confines of the cave, she was not happy at the thought that Joshua and herself would be inhaling secondary smoke. As though commanded to do so, he lay his cigarette paper and pouch aside. There was something more normal and responsive in him now, and she guessed that it was reality that he could not face and hence the need to float constantly on a cloud of drug-induced euphoria.

Now full and in a snug position, Joshua was quickly asleep.

"May I take him back to my husband, now?" she asked with a slight tremulo in her voice.

"What will happen to me?" he asked in return as though a new level of awareness had invaded his thoughts.

"I wish I could answer that. I do care what happens to you—I want you to know that."

He reached out and touched her cheek, and in a moment both of their eyes had grown misty again.

"May I go now?" she asked again after a moment.

"Yes. Take your son and go."

She reached once more into the diaper bag and extracted a blanket. She wrapped her child and lifted him to her shoulder. There was no waking him this time. He slept as soundly as a hibernating bear. She started toward the cave opening, and Tufarelli followed.

Long before they'd reached the breastworks, the brightening light of day had penetrated farther into the cave's mouth. The sun was now nine o'clock high, and it was as though she walked into a bright spotlight. From afar, there would be those awaiting her appearance on stage, but she hoped Tufaelli didn't have the same thought. If he did, would he reach for one of the weapons she could see stacked against the breastworks?

Once at the protective wall, she started to lay Joshua along the top while she climbed over, but Tufarelli took the child from her hands. A dart of fear ran through her in his action, but she smiled at him and said, "Thank you."

When she'd climbed over and her feet were on firm ground again, she held out her arms and he relinquished the child to her. She turned to go, and to her startled amazement he climbed over the breastworks also and came to her side. She let her eyes adjust to the bright light for a moment, took a few steps, and then she saw them. To each side of the cave opening with their backs pressed firmly against the stone wall stood four state troopers, their revolvers drawn. She froze in her tracks, not knowing whether she was supposed to run or to move out very normally. She sensed in an instant Tufarelli's impending death, and she rebelled at the thought. On the stone roof directly above the opening, a fifth trooper lay on his belly, the barrel of a revolver pointing to the ground. Before Tufarelli stepped too far into the open, she darted to his side. He seemed to sense in her rapid pivot the threat of danger, but he made no quick move to seek the protection of his stone fortress. He took another step toward her side and looked about. He studied at length the face of each law officer present. As though his curiosity was now satisfied, he looked back into her eyes. No terror had gripped him, no tenseness registered across his frail body. Perhaps he had faced drawn guns so often that he was numbed to the effect. Nobody moved. They all seemed frozen in time.

"They're going to take me back to the hospital, aren't they?"

"Yes, but soon you'll be well again. When you've recovered, would you like to come and see Joshua?

"Yes, I'd like that."

"His father works in the mine all day, and maybe when Joshua's older, you'd enjoy coming in the afternoon and playing ball with him. We have a nice flat piece of ground, and it'll make an ideal ball field."

Nothing more came from his lips. He looked once more into her eyes and nodded. He stepped aside, and she saw the spirit go out of him. His frail body slumped, and he crossed his hands behind his back as though he had just agreed to become a prisoner of war. Her eyes flooded once more as she saw the officers step forth and apply handcuffs.

Only when she had walked off and started across the ravine floor did she notice that the far perimeter was obliterated behind a smoke screen. As she hurried her steps and sucked in more air, she began to cough. She tucked the blanket around Joshua's face more carefully to filter the air before it reached his nostrils. High up on the mountain behind where she'd stood calling out to Tufarelli, she could see leaping flames and trees belching smoke, licking ever closer. She tried hurrying her steps still more, but twice she almost fell as rolling stones under her feet gave way. If Joe and Dowless and the others could see her coming at all, it must appear as though she now walked through a fog. No sooner had she thought this than she saw through the haze her beloved husband leading a band of men toward her.

Before they reached her, she heard a helicopter round the mountain, drop through a cloud bank, and come in low for an approach up the floor of the ravine. Now she was laughing and crying and trying to run all at the same time, and in a few more moments she had sailed into Joe's arms. He crushed her to him with such force that their sleeping child cried out a protest at having his sleep interrupted.

"Save the tears for later," Dowless called out. "We've got to get out of here! The fire ring is within 300 yards of closing."

The chopper eased along the ravine floor, its rescue basket already lowered and swinging. As she hurried toward it, Maria saw Dowless and Stanford steady the pendulous object for her seating. When she was safely strapped in, she said, "I want Joe to come with me. You think the big hunk, added to my weight, would sink the ship?"

"Not a chance," Dowless said. "We'll send him up behind you."

Once inside the belly of the great bird, Maria held Joshua tightly and leaned over. There was a childish thrill in seeing her man being lifted from the ground. There was an irony in it after all; it was as though they three had mounted the back of a great eagle who would soon wing them southward to the sanctuary of their own nest.